SHERLO[ ]

MW00334519

MYSTERY MAGAZINE

VOL. 7, NO. 7   **Issue #28**

"IM SORRY, SIR, BUT I CAN'T POISON YOUR WIFE, AS SHE'S ASKED ME TO POISON YOU."

STAFF

Publisher: *John Betancourt*
Editor: *Marvin Kaye*
Assistant Editors: *Sam Hogan, Karl Würf,* and *Steve Coupe*

✗

Sherlock Holmes Mystery Magazine is published by Wildside Press, LLC. Single copies: $10.00 + $3.00 postage. U.S. subscriptions: $59.95 (postage paid) for the next 6 issues in the U.S.A., from: Wildside Press LLC, Subscription Dept. 7945 MacArthur Blvd, Suite 215, Cabin John, MD 20818. International subscriptions: see our web site at www.wildsidepress.com. Available as an ebook through all major ebook etailers, or our web site, wildsidepress.com.

FROM WATSON'S NOTEBOOKS

My colleague Mr Kaye informs me that several readers have written to *Sherlock Holmes Mystery Magazine* to ask how it is possible that Holmes and I from the periods of Victorian and Edwardian England are still alive and functioning more than a century later. The answer is both interesting, I believe, and certainly shows my friend's forward thinking. It had not occurred to me to explain, but Holmes urges me to do so. Therefore I shall set pen to paper (yes, I still prefer longhand!) and in the near future will set forth the remarkable circumstances of our longevity.

This issue features the fascinating case that I wrote long ago of the Beryl Coronet and I have permitted Mr Lee Enderlin to peruse my notes on "The Problem of the Vanishing Bullet," an adventure that at one point rather pleased Inspector Lestrade, though shall we say he was a little off the mark.

And now here are a few thoughts from my colleague and coeditor.

⤫ ⤫ ⤫ ⤫

Of the many stories in this issue of *Sherlock Holmes Mystery Magazine*, I was especially taken by Sanford Zane Meschkow's "Pennwood Avenue," which has been in our fiction inventory for far too long. Our regular cartoonist Marc Bilgrey also offers a new story of his own: "Motive," plus new tales by Michael Hemmingson, Laird Long, Dan Andriacco, and Gary Lovisi (among others)

In addition to Dr Watson's promised longevity explanation, our 28th issue welcomes back many of our regular authors and several talented newcomers.

Canonically Yours,
Marvin Kaye

COMING NEXT TIME...

STORIES! ARTICLES!
SHERLOCK HOLMES & DR. WATSON!

Sherlock Holmes Mystery Magazine #29
is just a few months away...watch for it!

ASK MRS HUDSON

(Mrs) Martha Hudson

Now that Spring is upon us, it's nice to have a few warm sunny days interspersed with our English rain. Does it ever stop raining in England? It may not seem so, but I promise you, we do see the sun. And there is something particularly refreshing about the Spring rain — it washes London clean, I believe. It should also water the pansies and snowdrops which are now making their appearance in my garden. Granted, there isn't much space for gardening at 221 Baker Street, but it is such a British occupation that I cannot avoid getting my hands in the dirt once Winter has gone. I am careful to wash up and have the floors swept before Mr Holmes gets home, however; I do not need to know the particular composition of every inch of ground and I *do* remember it from one year to the next, thank you very much!

This brings me to our first letter, from Leonora J, a lady living in Bexhill-on-Sea:

> Dear Mrs Hudson,
>
> I must admit to having two passions in life: reading Dr Watson's exciting stories and gardening. Do either Sherlock Holmes or the esteemed Doctor enjoy gardening? If so, I can send them some choice cuttings from my summer beds.

Well, if Mrs J does enjoy my lodgers's adventures, it surely must have been awhile since she's read them, else she would remember that Dr Watson once graded Mr Holmes's knowledge of botany as "variable," with no knowledge of "practical gardening," although that depends on what one considers "practical," as you shall read. It is also common knowledge that while Sherlock Holmes may not be the most religious of men, he does, in a transcendental fashion, find evidence of the Divine in nature, particularly in flowers, of which roses and violets are his favorites.

Now Dr Watson does like flowers, as gentlemen do, but he mostly sees them as a way to gain favour with the ladies. Many is the time I've found gaps among my daffodils, tulips, marguerites, pinks and even on my rose bush when he's been courting. I suppose I shouldn't mind, provided one of his suits were successful, but I often believe the doctor enjoys the chase rather more than the prize itself. No one, I fear, can live up to the memories of his Mary.

Sherlock Holmes, however, seems to have taken his friend's description to heart and does now and again do some gardening. The summer after he first moved into 221B, in fact, I found him digging up my hyacinths. I grabbed him straight by his right ear I did, pulling him up and demanding just what he imagined he was doing! He looked so comical, standing there, rubbing his ear with a grubby hand and looking shame-faced as a little boy that I did forgive him, but told him that I would absolutely *not* permit him to grow belladonna and monk's-hood in *my* beds! The next morning I was awakened by the most horrible din on my rooftop and after putting on my dressing gown and slippers, I climbed upstairs to find him building a hothouse, of all things, with Dr Watson as his assistant. Now I love my boys, but I must say I had doubts about the, erm, durability of any structure they might build. Fortunately, my fears proved ill-founded. Mr Holmes has found a home for his poisonous plants where they are safe from my hoe, nibbling animals, and Heaven forbid, curious children. What does he plant there, you ask? Just about any lethal plant you can imagine: foxglove, hemlock, gelsemium, tansy, laurel … far too many to count, I fear. He once told Dr Watson that he might use some to compound his own medications, but the doctor prefers to prescribe medicines, rather than to make them himself.

My column on my lodgers's arrival on Baker Street inspired some curiosity in Miss Thomasina Ford, who writes from Malmesbury, Wiltshire:

> Dear Mrs Hudson,
>
> Could you tell us how Sherlock Holmes got his early cases? I know that Dr Watson says people came to their flat and he solved their problems and got paid for it, but how did they know to come to see him in the first place? My uncle lives in London and he says that he never saw an advert for Sherlock Holmes, Private Inquiry Agent in any paper.

Well, dear, I must first say that Mr Holmes is not a "Private Inquiry Agent" but a "Consulting Detective." Much like a consulting physician, he is called when a particular case is beyond the skill of general practitioners — in this case, those practitioners being the local police or Scotland Yard.

But the question of advertising is an interesting one, as you do see advertisements for detectives in the papers, generally one on top of the other beneath the "Agony columns." Now, of course, Mr Holmes is a household name, thanks to his remarkable gifts (and Dr Watson's stories), but it wasn't always so and he has told me that, as a young man just starting out, he wondered how he should attract business. He did consider advertising, however, if you remember, this was the time when the Scotland Yard detectives who were convicted of conspiring with the criminals Benson and Kurr to obstruct justice in the matter of illicit gambling businesses, having been released from prison, began to try to re-enter society by offering their services as private inquiry agents. Mr Holmes did not fancy having his name grouped in the papers with those of Mr Meiklejohn, Mr Clarke or Mr Druscovich and I do not blame him. He once told me that as he was just getting established, Mr Meiklejohn offered him a job as one of his foreign agents. He could use Mr Holmes's knowledge of French and his connections in that country, he said. Now Mr Holmes has always wanted to make his own way in the world and has no desire to be yoked to any employer, but he also told me that he sensed something a bit *devious* about Meiklejohn. "Druscovich and Clarke were fools," he said, "But they might have gone on in their careers with honour had they not fallen in with Inspector Meiklejohn." As he considered the question of whether he should advertise, he also imagined what he should like his future to be.

"Although I knew that at least some of my early work would be taken up with finding lost items, missing relatives and divorce work — the stock in trade of most detectives — I knew that my talents were worthy of more. If I wished to be a true professional — a *consultant* — then I had to behave like one from the start. Everyone knows that members of the professions — legal and medical—do not advertise; it is unseemly and those who do are regarded as hacks and quacks. By beginning as I wished to end, I do believe that I enabled my rise."

Without advertising, he had to work very hard for his early clients. Every morning he would go out and buy as many papers as he could afford, often picking up discarded ones from coffee shops and train stations. He would then peruse the Agony columns and the criminal news, looking for problems and cases in which he thought he could offer assistance. With the public, his success in offering advice in family and financial matters, as well as his skill in finding missing valuables and people, led to his name being passed about in all quarters as that of a man of discernment and discretion. When he offered his help in police cases, his deductions and most of all, his refusal to take credit for them, served to ingratiate him to enough constables and inspectors that the police soon knew to call him sooner, rather than later. Now, of course, he can afford to take only those cases which interest him, but I do think he occasionally misses those days when the uncertainty of it all added a bit of excitement to his endeavours.

And now, my dears, I think I shall go make some calls in this wonderful weather before it decides to rain again. Dr Watson paints me as a homebody, but I am actually out and about quite a lot! Before I go, however, I shall give you a recipe and a joke.

First the joke, which of all people, *my* readers will most appreciate:

He: "Oh, yes, when I was in London I was enthusiastically received in court circles."
She: "Really? What was the charge against you?"

⚔ ⚔ ⚔ ⚔

And this makes a lovely dish for Spring:

LAMB CUTLETS WITH MINT SAUCE

For lamb and marinade:
6 lamb chops, cut and trimmed
salt and pepper to taste
4 large tbs of fresh mint, chopped
1 tbs moist sugar
4 tbs of vinegar

For mint sauce:
2 tbs moist sugar
4 tbs of vinegar

Preparation:
Mix together the mint, sugar and vinegar in a large bowl. Dust the chops with salt and pepper, then place them in the bowl and cover them with the sauce for an hour, turning once or twice. Afterwards, place chops on a griddle (do not wipe) and cook. Pour the sauce that is left into a saucepan with two more tbs of sugar and 4 tbs of vinegar. Let it boil up once, then serve it in a sauce boat. Dish the cutlets on a bed of mashed potatoes and send to the table very hot.

✗

THREE "BUCKET" MYSTERIES

A REVIEW

Eugene D. Goodwin

Anthony Berkeley: *Trial and Error*
Leo Perutz: *The Master of the Day of Judgment*
Stuart Turton: *The Seven ½ Deaths of Evelyn Hardcastle*

Recently I encountered the third of the three novels listed above. Upon reading it, I knew I had to review it for *Sherlock Holmes Mystery Magazine* and as long as I meant to do so, I thought I should add two more mysteries that are in their own way as unique.

Anthony Berkeley (1893-1971) was a prolific British mystery writer who wrote under several names, including Anthony Berkeley—his full name was Anthony Berkeley Cox—as well as A. Monmouth Platts and Francis Iles. Perhaps best known for his series of Roger Sheringham novels, one of which is *The Poisoned Chocolates Case*, cited in Act One of Anthony Shaffer's play *Sleuth*.

While the posioned chocolates mystery is interesting in its own right, it is outstripped by *Trial and Error*, one of the most clever and unpredictable mysteries I've ever read. Not only is it ingeniously plotted with a wonderful protagonist, it also contains much sly understated humour.

Its central character Lawrence Todhunter is a fiftyish moderately wealthy gentleman who has done little with his life except write book reviews for a weekly London magazine whose principal is a friend. At a dinner party for a group of acquaintances, Todhunter proposes the hypothetical question, *If you knew you must die soon, what would you do to make your remaining time worthwhile?* To his amazement (with one abstention by a priest at the party) they say they'd find some terrible person who is making life miserable for good people and murder her or him, for if they are going to die, anyway, they do not fear the consequences of being caught.

What they don't know is that Todhunter's physician has told him that he has an aortic aneurism and cannot expect to live longer than a few more months, perhaps less or if he is very careful about his lifestyle, possibly as much as a year.

At first Todhunter does not intend to follow his friends's advice, but then he comes upon an actress who is ruining the lives of a family he knows. So eventually, of course, the murder takes place.

But then things go wrong. Todhunter has decided to take a long cruise where he will see things he never saw before and if he dies along the way, fine. But when he reaches Tokyo he discovers that an innocent man has been arrested for the murder. Of course he returns immediately to London to turn himself in … but the authorities regard him as a crank. They have their killer. The innocent man is soon tried and sentenced to be hanged.

Thus Todhunter must become a detective and uncover clues to prove that *I dunit!*

Which he does, but the police still won't take him seriously and since the criminal trial has already taken place, in a splendid further twist Todhunter must become involved in a *civil* trial to prove his guilt.

Trial and Error is a "fun read" and contains one further twist that I shall not spoil.

⨯ ⨯ ⨯ ⨯

Leo (Leopold) Perutz (1882-1957) was an Austrian critic, mathematician and novelist who wrote eleven unusual novels, some of them fantasies; two have not yet been translated into English. His work has been praised by such literary luminaries as Jorge Luis Borges, Anthony Boucher, Ian Fleming and Graham Greene. Karl Edward Wagner called *The Master of the Day of Judgment* (original title: *Der Meister des Jungsten Tages*) as one of the thirteen best non-supernatural horror novels (though it does skirt with the supernatural). The editor of *Sherlock Holmes Mystery Magazine* Marvin Kaye found a copy of the Collier Mystery Classics edition and was actually reading it on his honeymoon!

Anthony Boucher, editor of the Collier series, said this of Perutz's novel: "*The Master of the Day of Judgment* starts off as a formal period drama of Vienna in 1909, with officers and actors and adultery and horror—all suggestive of a play by Schnitzler. It shifts into a straight detective story, then into a tale of supernatural terror, then finally into an ending as Viennese as the beginning—if you recall that Vienna is the cradle of psychiatry. Like every story of Perutz's, it creates its own form and sets, rather than follows, precedents."

When I first read it, I could not accept its ending, but then I went back and reread it and found that its ending is well set up and positively inevitable. It is a rare performance when a genre novel is also a great work of art.

⨯ ⨯ ⨯ ⨯

Stuart Turton's *The Seven ½ Deaths of Evelyn Hardcastle* is a complex mystery, but it is also a fantasy and as one nears its end the reader discovers that it is science fiction as well. I came upon the American hardcover edition of this book several weeks ago and was fascinated by the favorable reviews quoted on it. The one that struck me as most interesting is one critic's characterization of it as (words approximate) 'Agatha Christie meets *Groundhog*

Day.' Though not entirely accurate—Turton's style is much more polished than most of Christie's works—it is a fair capsule of the unusualness of the book.

I did not buy it when I first came upon it because the price was more than I cared to pay, so I went online and discovered a much cheaper edition of the British paperback called *The Seven Deaths of Evelyn Hardcastle.* Why the title change? I consulted Turton's British agent and they explained that they learned that another U. S. book was being published: *The Seven Husbands of Evelyn Hugo* by Taylor Jenkins Reid. I thought it a good reason for the titular alteration and I think 7 ½ makes it more interesting, anyway.

The book is long (though never tedious) with a plot so complicated that it is best to read it with as few interruptions as possible. There are many characters; fortunately, at the beginning of the book a complete cast list is included. I referred to it often while reading.

The Christie-like aspect of *The Seven Deaths of Evelyn Hardcastle* is that the action takes place at Blackheath, a large decrepit estate that has been re-opened by Lady Helena Hardcastle on the twentieth anniversary of her son's murder. Many guests have been invited and the first night a masked ball will be held. At eleven p. m. Evelyn Hardcastle will be murdered.

From this point on, Turton's book bears no resemblance to a traditional mystery. One does not even know who the protagonist is for quite some time, though one assumes it is Doctor Sebastian Bell, whose actions are the focus of the first chapters. But it turns out that the real hero, so to speak, is Aiden Bishop, who finds himself trapped each day in the mind and body of one of the guests or staff members at the estate. He learns from a disguised "plague doctor" that several people, including Bishop, are meant to identify Evelyn Hardcastle's murderer before she is killed. If not, when the second day dawns Bishop has become a different person—*and Evelyn is alive again!!!*

Bishop is told he (and the other "sleuths") have eight days to identify the killer. If they do not the entire cycle will start all over again. However, among the guests—many of whom are dire scoundrels—is a footman who means to murder every one of the would-be detectives. As a matter of fact he does kill Bishop's host more than once, after which of course he wakes up trapped within another person.

Turton further complicates matters by not making the story's timeline linear. When we reach Day Four the story reverts to events on Day Two. Several times we go back and forth in such a manner.

The Seven Deaths of Evelyn Hardcastle is indeed an unusual, perhaps unique, mystery novel. Its characters are fascinating, its dialogue excellent, its setting described masterfully. And maybe you'll even figure it out, though I doubt it.

I certainly didn't.

✗

TWO CHEERS FOR DR WATSON

Janice Law

Sherlock Holmes is among the most famous characters ever created, known to literate folks around the globe. But while the creation of the cerebral sleuth was testament to Conan Doyle's skill, in some ways the crucial invention was not Sherlock, but Dr. Watson.

Consider that Sherlock was not the first of his type, being preceded by Edgar Allan Poe's C. Auguste Dupin and Emile Gaboriau's Monsieur Lecoq, although the Englishman was to have many more appearances in print than either. Consider, too, that while the "world's first consulting detective" has successors as famous as Hercule Poirot and Nero Wolfe, none has been able to dethrone him.

Why? I think the touch of genius was in the presentation of the detective and that Conan Doyle picked the ideal character as his narrator. Watson is intelligent—but not imaginative. He is observant of emotions and human reactions but weak on physical details. He is humane and sensible, a good doctor and a good man. If a little dull compared to Sherlock, Watson proves well worth the great detective's trust. He is reliable in a pinch. And so we believe him.

As we do another dull, reliable, unimaginative narrator who helped an almost exactly contemporary novella to world-wide fame and cultural status. I refer to Mr. Utterson, the really boring lawyer who narrates the first part of *The Strange Case of Dr. Jekyll and Mr. Hyde* by Conan Doyle's fellow Edinburgh Scot, Robert Louis Stevenson. By the time we realize that this upright, laconic, down-to-Earth bastion of the legal profession is telling us a totally bizarre and improbable tale, we have long since surrendered our disbelief.

Whether or not Conan Doyle picked up a cue from Mr. Utterson, Dr. Watson similarly makes Sherlock Holmes plausible, while standing in for the reader who may not see what is elementary to Holmes, either. Watson asks the questions the reader needs answered but he also adds far more to the narrative. His forthright opinions and honest geniality are a foil for the often deliberately cryptic Holmes. At the same time, his role as narrator enables Holmes to be just as mysterious as he likes.

Consider for a minute how different the stories would be—and I think how much less attractive—had their creator settled on Holmes as a first person narrator. If the detective was reporting what he was observing, the reader could hardly be kept in suspense. Watson, who is often mystified by the detective's peculiar method, describes Holmes's actions but misses his insights, thus keeping us mystified and intrigued, too.

And then Watson is a much nicer person. He is fascinated by his friend but by no means blind to his vanity and arrogance, traits which on constant display would no doubt be irritating. But they are not on constant display. As readers we have to do with Watson, who, while he will never solve the cases, leavens the calculations, the obsession with data and the rather cold-bloodedness of his companion. In the process, he creates the atmosphere which is one of the charms of the stories.

Holmes, of course, does not approve. He rebuked Watson's first attempt, a small pamphlet composed to see that he received credit for a difficult case (*A Study in Scarlet*), as an attempt to insert romance into the exact science of detection. This is a fault as great as "...if you had worked a love story or an elopement into the fifth proposition of Euclid."

Watson, no doubt thinking of the mysterious deaths, wild frontier adventures, the exotic habits of the Mormon pioneers and the lover's revenge that marked the case, protests that "the romance was there". To which Sherlock replies, "Some facts should be suppressed" and claims that the only point that deserved mention was his "analytical reasoning".

No wonder Watson feels a bit hard done by and notes not only his friend's egotism but spots the "small vanity" under his "quiet and didactic manner". Too much of Sherlock Holmes would not be a good thing.

Of course, Conan Doyle could, like that other great master of eccentrics, Charles Dickens, have favored an omniscient narrator and given us Holmes uncut, so to speak. This tack, however, loses the great advantage of companionship. Prior to Watson, the consulting detective had useful acquaintances like the Baker Street Irregulars and Toby's owner, but they are acquaintances, not friends. Sherlock keeps the Irregulars at some little distance, by preference negotiating with Wiggins, their leader, and instructing the rest to remain downstairs. He communicates with Mr. Sherman only when he needs the dog. Holmes is liked and admired but lacks the loyal, but not uncritical, support of a real friend like Watson.

Minus Watson we would lose another of the charms of the stories, the atmosphere of masculine coziness created by the rooms in Baker Street. The litter of books and papers, tobacco smoke, Holmes's laboratory, the cheerful fire, the fine breakfasts and dinners produced by the efficient but mostly invisible Mrs. Hudson are in sharp contrast to the London weather without, almost uniformly foggy and chilly with driving rain a distinct possibility.

Here is a comfortable life without many of the frictions of daily living. There are no domestic dramas—except maybe the good doc's attempts to moderate Holmes's drug consumption—few responsibilities, no boss and no nine-to-five. It's ideal really and all it needs is a nice case of murder, blackmail, or reckless endangerment to make life sweet.

The Sherlock Holmes stories have charm, atmosphere, the joys of friendship, plus the mental stimulation and occasional dangers of detection. No wonder the stories have lasted, but don't give all the credit to Holmes.

✗

LH'S LEGACY

Rochelle Campbell

He took two drags on his stogie. The posh surrounding was beginning to grate on his nerves. He was down two grand and just put up two more; the two he borrowed from Lefty to tide him over until he got a gig.

Shit.

Lefty, across from him, flicked down a pair of ladies.

It took all of his willpower not to reach over and snatch back his money. But this wasn't *that* kind of party. Here, everything was played by the rules. Nice and pat.

Damn. My first real game since I got out of the joint and it had to be a privy Strip invite-only game.

"Are you in or out?" asked the dealer.

Lefty shifted in his seat and sent Hefty a *Don't-make-me-regret-I-got-you-invited* look.

Stan "Hefty" Beaumont didn't bother to glare back.

Damnit! How the hell am I going to survive for the next month? I can't go back to the Big House. I just can't!

A single drop of sweat rolled from under his spunky purple fedora down his neck. Hefty didn't think anyone noticed, but leaned back a bit to stop the errant water from flowing further down his back. That's when he remembered *his* ace in the hole.

While incarcerated, Little Hands a.k.a. LH, one of his block mates, told him about a scam he pulled on a rich dame that he'd off'd a bit too soon and got caught because of his hastiness. The part of the scam that Hefty liked was how LH painstakingly created a tunnel in the thickest part of the heel of his shoe. That's where he burrowed the extra slim scalpel in a fiberglass lined slot that he covered with an undistinguishable plug of material similar to the shoe's sole.

With all of that preparation, LH killed the broad, grabbed the money and forgot to put the murder weapon in its hiding place and left it at the scene of the crime!

Hefty seized upon the idea; he figured if he created a secret slot like that for an Ace or a Joker if he ever got in a bind he could ease out the surefire card and walk away with none the wiser.

To keep his mind occupied during the six months before his parole date, Hefty worked out the schematics of how to construct the slot in the sole of a shoe, what the proper height of the heel should be, the width and which material would be best. All this he worked out knowing that a day like today would inevitably happen.

"In? Or out?" the dealer asked testily.

Hefty took off his fedora, set it on his lap and brought the left foot of his purple suede and alligator shoes with the customized midnight blue rubber soles up a few inches. He cleared his throat as he brushed some imaginary dust from his pristine shoes, or so it looked to the others.

Hefty sighed heavily, stood up as if he were about to pack it in, shook his head in negation and banged his large hands onto the table jostling chips, money and shot glasses. Then said in a dejected tone, "In," before dropping ungracefully back into his seat; his right hand was still on the table. The other well-dressed men grunted knowing the look and sound of resignation only too well. The dealer flicked a card towards Hefty.

Hefty moved quick, bending his head overly much in the process, so intent on the dealer's card and the upcoming switch.

Only the guy on Hefty's left cared when the hat fell, or so Hefty thought.

"Here, Bub," he said tossing the fedora on the table. It landed on top of Hefty's right hand the one that covered the card the dealer just dealt. Hefty's mind and fingers moved quickly.

"Thanks, Charlie."

Nimbly, Hefty slid the card the dealer gave him into his sleeve and picked up the hat with his left hand placing it back at its jaunty angle, then folded his arms across his chest.

He let a slow smile steal over his face when everyone stared at the table and saw his final hand.

He'd just won $20G's.

Hefty felt the weight of the shocked stares as the tension in the room ratcheted up. Hefty kept his cool and refused to look anyone in the eye except the dealer. To him he nodded his thanks.

The dealer looked at Lefty, and the others and gave a slow nod. "That's his win, fellas."

With a gleam in his eye Hefty chomped down on his stoogie. He nodded to all in the room before taking up his winnings, pocketing the three large stacks of bills and leaving with a pep in his step.

Hefty knew that he'd better get rid of the switched-out card as soon as he got clear of the joint. He *knew* he should. But he just had to see what it was!

✗ ✗ ✗ ✗

Charlie's eye twitched as he watched Hefty go. He had seen the stark naked fear in Hefty's eyes. Saw the light of inspiration, followed by the wicked gleam of avarice in Hefty's pale green eyes. Charlie knew something wasn't right.

Too busy arranging to have Miss Dahlia's best escort as his companion for the night, Hefty didn't bother to throw away the card, much less check what it was on his way home. He waited until he was fully checked into the penthouse suite, then waited a bit more until well after the bellhop was tipped before he pulled the card out of his sleeve. Some part of him enjoyed the sweet torture.

It was an *Ace*!

Hefty roared with laughter at the irony of it. He would have won, anyway! He grinned on his way to the bathroom, finally intent on destroying the evidence.

There was a knock at the door. Feeling invincible, he shoved the card in his trouser pocket and went to answer the knock. Two hotel security guards were there along with Charlie, who said, "Check his pockets!"

Charlie had a nasty knowing grin on his face.

Hefty was frisked and they found the card and he heard those dreaded words, yet again, "You have the right to remain silent…"

✗

ROOKER

Laird Long

It was a dive off B Street. A dingy, dirty bar filled with sweaty, stinking men yelling and laughing and swearing, drinking copiously. Where there's water, there's booze.

Voltumus had plenty of water, deep beneath its sun-seared surface. Thanks to an ancient Ice Age that had long ago melted into the planet's cracks and crevices. And now Voltumus had plenty of 'drips', the roughnecks shipped out from Earth to drill and pipe and tank the cool, crystal-clear water, barge it back to an increasingly parched home planet. Watertown was the center of it all, a boomtown in the middle of a vast and desolate nowhere, a rugged oasis.

My drip was crowded up against the brass-railed bar that ran the length of one side of the stifling room. He was shoulder-to-shoulder with other broad-shouldered cohorts, yet strangely all by himself. He'd take a sip from his shotglass, then fling the lethal moon mash down his throat. Like he was building up the courage to do something out of character, perhaps out of bounds.

I watched him from a tiny round table in the corner, smoke and alcohol fumes blurring my vision. My table rocked with the bodies of men stumbling or shoving against it, so I held my drink in my hand, untouched.

Kit Misker finally set his latest empty shotglass down and pushed away from the bar, mind seemingly made up. He elbowed his way through the raucous throng, to the saloon-style swing doors, out into the night. I followed, getting challenged to more than one fight as I muscled my way clear of the room. Voltumus was a hostile environment, and it showed in its inhabitants.

The street was almost as packed as the bar. It was Saturday, pay had been distributed, and the drips were sloshing their money around before they returned to the dunes and the underground, on Monday. Misker made his way along B Street to the canopied entrance of the Hotel Largo. He glanced right, left, stared straight ahead at the heavy, frosted glass doors of the joint.

The Hotel Largo was five storeys of sandstone brick and pulsing pleasure. The ground floor was lit up neon-bright and noisy, the others floors sporting shade-drawn windows that leaked just a little light, but throbbed with excitement. It was a brothel, thirty rookers or so inside to choose from.

I leaned against an undertaker's storefront window and waited for Misker to make his move, one way or the other. The tall, curly-haired man with the hangdog expression and brown, puppy dog eyes at last gulped his protruding Adam's apple and walked forward, pushed through the front doors of the brothel.

"Pleasure dreams," I murmured, mouthing the Hotel Largo's blazing red signage.

I cooled my heels while Misker heated his loins. I'd have to break the bad news to his jealous wife back on Earth. She'd hired me to find out if her drip was cheating on her way out in the galaxial wastelands. And she hadn't differentiated between real women, of which there were few, and rookers, of which there were more. She was the possessive type, a rooker as good, or bad, as the real thing.

For most, it was a fine line: was having sex with a robot-hooker actually cheating? They weren't humans, after all, just shrewdly crafted along those lines. I pulled a deck of cigs out of my jacket pocket, shook one out, getting all philosophical. Never a wise thing to do in Watertown.

Sure enough, a beefy hand slapped my cig away, another huge mitt jarring the deck down to the ground. My arms were clasped in twin vises. "Tenn Galon wants to see you, Diamond," one of the thugs growled.

They were big men, even for Watertown. They walked me over to a vehicle waiting by the curb, and we all got in as a threesome.

"I'm not swilling enough moon at Tenn Galon's joints, that it?" I cracked, when the vehicle hit zoom.

Their faces were as cool and blank as the sky. I let it and me ride.

✗ ✗ ✗ ✗

"I don't give a damn what your business is! You're working for me now!" Tenn Galon jabbed a sausage finger down at me for emphasis, blowing smoke and garlic.

The notorious business, brothel, and bargain game owner-operator towered over me in my chair. His round face was filmed with grease and sweat, like everything he touched, his corpulent body encased in a tuxedo that strained its stitching and his credibility.

His office was opulent in a blatantly obvious way, filled with expensive items like the woman standing in back of his football field-sized desk. She was blonde and sleek, decked out in a shiny silver dress and a stunning array of jewellery. She watched the proceedings with a bland expression on her aristocratic face, her green eyes burning dully.

"You don't have any right to hijack me off the street and into your operations," I protested, for show more than effect. "I—"

"Shut your hole! Two-bit gumshoes don't tell me what I can't do—not on this or any planet!" His beady blue eyes glared down at me out of his fat-laden face.

I sat back in the chair, waited. At least I was still alive. Many of those called upon for conference with the galactic gangster never surfaced again, or so I'd heard. The sands of Voltumus ran deep, I'd been told.

Tenn Galon swivelled around, his skin-tight tuxedo and black leather shoes squeaking. "Out!" he barked at the woman.

She shrugged. Then slipped through a side door in a lithe, flowing motion that captured the room's attention.

Tenn Galon was back on top of me. "One of my rooker's been stole!"

I raised an eyebrow.

"Ebony. Cost me a cool million! The latest and greatest model—fully functional." He gestured obscenely with his hands. "I can't get a replacement from Earth for another six months. I'd use the missus," he jerked a thumb at the door where the blonde had made her exit, "but, unfortunately, she's a real woman." He hacked out a phlegmy laugh.

Prostitution was semi-legal on Voltumus, but only if robots were employed.

"What do you—"

"I want you to find Ebony, get her back! Then I'll take care of the asswipes who stole her." He turned and rumbled around his desk, sat down in his shiny brown leather chair in a whoosh of stale air. "I hear you're pretty good at jobs like that. And since you was on Voltumus anyway…" He hefted his hamhocks and grinned.

"Who do you—"

"Bim Starrett or Sedge Mackey. They run the other joy houses in town." He pursed his mouthflaps. "Tough part's going to be making sure it's her. See, with these newer models, you can even better change their eyes and hair and skin. Their tit size, too, of course. Even their body shape and length."

He grunted, his pig's eyes gleaming with obvious fond remembrances of Ebony. Then he pointed at me again. "But that's your job—to figure out how to find her and get her back. Hedge'll help you."

He looked at the screen on his desk. Our meeting was over.

✗ ✗ ✗ ✗

Hedge was a house mechanic. Every brothel had one; a computer and mechanical whiz who kept the machinery of commerce functioning, maintaining and repairing rookers. Some of the customers could be a little rough on the merchandise, and there was always normal wear and tear, and bugs of a non-medical kind.

Tenn Galon's number one mechanic was a gnarled gnome of a man with a twisted grin and sense of humor. "Maybe you should test-drive 'em all, huh?" he quipped. "There're only about five hundred spread out in fifteen different houses."

"Did Ebony have any 'tells'? Pull to the right or anything like that?"

Hedge chortled. "Naw. That's old-school, early-model. Ebony had eight distinct personalities, from shy to sultry, all designed to give pleasure. She didn't have any flaws."

That was the thing about rookers, the way they were built: their personalities had to be friendly, accommodating. They couldn't pout or mope or get angry or murderous. In that respect, they weren't like real woman at all.

ı glanced around Hedge's workshop. It was in the basement of Tenn Galon's brothel on F Street, the Okay! Corral. The claustrophobic room was cluttered with computers and tools, pornographic holograms projected all over the place. And against one wall, six actual rookers were lined up, five females and one male, naked and turned-off. Their unseeing eyes glittered obscenely in the light, their bodies shining so.

Hedge scuttled over to an ivory-skinned, big-breasted brunette with wide violet eyes and lips as red and plush as rose petals. He grinned perversely at me, then pointed and clicked a remote control. The rooker shuddered to life, her long, dark eyelashes fluttering and sensual mouth opening, her body softening, breathing.

Hedge's stumpy fingers danced on the remote, and the rooker's hair went from black to blonde to red, long to short, eyes brown and then blue, skin pale to olive to black, breasts pumping up huge, body rising up taller. "You'll never find Ebony," the mechanic drooled. "Their BIN's are easily removed and replaced. That's so they can be easily stolen—so the manufacturers can sell more units. But their software—what really runs them—is proprietary, of course." He frowned like a petulant teenager. "Even I can't hack into it, to make 'em really unique."

The rooker was now caressing Hedge's face, and other working parts due south.

"We're going to have to wait for them to steal another one, then," I grated.

Hedge looked at me, his expression sublime. "What'll that accomplish?"

"In the old West it was called rustling. Know how they stopped it?"

Hedge nestled into the rooker's arms, settling his head down on her rising and falling breasts. "Hanging?"

"Branding."

Two weeks after I'd been shanghaied by Tenn Galon, another of his rookers turned up missing: Angelica, a blue-eyed blonde with pixiesque features, for all those were worth in identification. Also going missing at the same time, perhaps coincidentally but probably not, was Tenn Galon's wife.

I went on the prowl.

The Filly Ranch was located on the outskirts of Watertown, where the dust met the desert. It was one of Sedge Mackey's brothels. The western motif shot straight through to the white cowgirl hats the rookers wore, the silver six-shooters slung seductively from their bare hips.

Clementine was a bubbly, fun-loving redhead with a Dixie accent and a smile as big as all Texas. I crowded her up against a wall of our loving pen on the second floor before she even had a chance to unlatch her chaps, unholster my gun. I thrust my tongue into her open mouth and swirled it around inside, scouring her gums in back of her front teeth with the curled tip of my sticker. My oral explorations yielded no small T.

That's what Hedge and I had come up with: a small T branded just above the upper gumline in back of the rookers' front teeth. We knew whoever was rustling Tenn Galon's joy toys would go over the sophisticated stolen equipment with a fine-tooth scanner, or get his mechanic to do so, looking for any distinguishing exterior marks or under-skin identifiers, eliminating moles, birthmarks, and giveaway signs of stress and strain as required. And a rebuilt remote control would render the rooker sufficiently changed in other physical appearance for their camouflaging purposes. But it would have to be a really thorough, or kinky, house mechanic who searched in behind the upper front teeth for a tiny identifying brand.

I let go of Clementine and sat down on the bed, flared a cig.

"Why, honey, I hope that ain't all you got to offer a gal!?"

Her teeth shone like a constellation of lone stars, her grey eyes beaming with western hospitality. She dropped the white leather chaps, eager to please, built for it in the truest sense of the phrase. All rookers were programmed to be willing and able, compliant with any human desire, all of the time. Only this time, her considerable charm was wasted.

When she strolled over to me in her cowgirl boots, her breasts bouncing like overstuffed saddlebags, I switched her off. The room remote wasn't just for working the bed and screen.

✗ ✗ ✗ ✗

I worked my way across town, from west to east. By the time I hit the Hotsheet Motel on Pipeline Road, the plastic chit Tenn Galon had given me was running dangerously low on credit. I'd probed more females with tongue or finger in three days and nights than a gynaecologist does in a month. It was a dirty job, but someone had to do it, I guess.

And I'd like to say that I carried my part off strictly professionally, testing the merchandise for markage and then moving on. But if I left a room in under the thirty minimum bought and allotted minutes, suspicions would be aroused. I had to kill time somehow. I found a way.

So, when I pushed through the roadside glass office doors of the Hotsheet Motel, I was more than a little worn out.

This place was owned by Bim Starrett. It was done up low-track sleazy, a one-storey horseshoe loop of twenty rooms connected to the front office. The flaky paint scheme was yellow and red, the rooms threadbare, the beds creaky, the sheets hot as advertised.

Taylor was tall and skinny and tanlined, dressed for cheap thrills in a purple tubetop and pair of pink shorty-shorts. Her blonde, black-rooted hair was a fluffy mess, her warpaint garish. Her mouth hung loose as her joints. She was everything you'd expect to find and pay for in a motel like that, open for business all hours.

"So, how you want it, big boy?" she slurred, Mae West-style.

I grasped her arms and pulled her close. She groaned when I kissed her, moaned when I thrust my tongue into her mouth and curled it upwards.

I groaned. Nada.

ᴜ for the door, getting suddenly weary of the grind.

ᴄ grabbed my arm and spun me around. "What the fuck! Is that all you ᴳot!?"

I stared at her. Taylor's heavily made-up face had darkened with rage.

"Sorry, sweetheart, but I've got miles to go before I sleep with yet another rooker."

I shook off her claw and exited, bumping into Cindy on the sidewalk outside. She was placidly bringing some dirty sheets to the front office. But when we touched skin, she went into full seduction mode.

Her shtick was little girl lost, her overripe body on shameful display in a white shirt tied up at the front and a ruffled plaid skirt that barely came down to her thighs. She toed the concrete with a patent-leather shoe tip, her brown pigtails bobbing, eyes and braces glinting softly in the harsh light as she glanced up at me.

Eschewing the preliminaries, I stuck a finger in her mouth. She eagerly sucked on it. And I touched paydirt—the small T brand! "We're going home, sweetie," I rasped. And I joyously meant the both of us, the blue ball of Earth blazing in my memory.

Cindy blinked her liquid-brown eyes. "Back to my room, sir?"

It just wasn't in her programming to go anywhere else. So I manually switched her off, slung her over my shoulder. The door to Room 20 opened up and Taylor glared at me. I blew her kiss and spun around and strode forward. Right into the broad waiting chests of two male motel employees. "That's the guy," Taylor sneered.

"Takin' little Cindy for a walk?" one of the men asked.

"Dine-in only, pal," the other man growled.

They formed a solid wall of muscle, blocking my path and seriously jeopardizing my future.

I did a slow half-turn and dumped Cindy up against Taylor. "Okay, okay," I said, nice and easy. "No harm done." Yet.

I clenched my hands into fists and whirled around, hit the man on my right full in the face, knocking him backwards. I sunk a left hook into the other guy's gut, doubling him over. Followed that up with a kick to the jaw, toppling him onto the pavement. His cement head cracked on the concrete.

The other man charged me with open arms. I avoided his crushing embrace with a well-timed foot to the groin, leaving him retching. Then I brought my right fist up from my knees and shattered it and his chin. Only I cried out, though, because my assailant was out cold, joining his buddy in enforced slumber on the ground.

I scooped Cindy back up onto my shoulder, preparatory to rushing her over to my vehicle and zooming back to the relative safety of Tenn Galon's office. But a pointed boot-tip tripped me up. I staggered forward, spun around.

"Mrs. Tenn Galon, I presume?"

The scowling female in the purple tubetop and pink shorty-shorts confirmed my suspicions by spitting in my face, trying to claw my eyes out. I clicked a short left off the point of her chin and her eyes flickered like candles. I caught her up, draped her over my other shoulder, and shuffled fast and furious for my vehicle.

"You helped Bim Starrett steal the rookers?" I said more than asked, when we were all safely zooming away from the battleground and stolen property depot known as the Hotsheet Motel. Tenn Galon's wife was in the front seat with me, Cindy in the back.

"We were going to be partners!" she retorted, rubbing her jaw. "Which is more than Tenn Galon would ever let me become."

"Then why were you working the rooms?"

She looked at me, her eyes glittering defiantly. "For compassion, for empathy, for love! What a woman needs!"

I stared at her.

She shook her head. "You wouldn't understand. In a world of rookers, what chance does a real woman have? All females are property, objects, as far as men like Tenn Galon are concerned—not people." She brushed a couple of fingers under her nose. "And he'd rather get his pleasure from a rooker. They don't give him any backtalk, or demand anything of him. And there's more variety."

She blinked, tears in her eyes. "So I take my feelings where I can get them. The customers give me tenderness…and longing."

She almost had me crying.

But then her voice changed, back to the way it'd sounded when she was putting the finger on me. "And they give me money."

I snorted.

She suddenly pressed against me. A warm, slim arm coiled around my neck, a soft, slender hand sliding up onto my chest, then lower, where the crux of the matter lay with most men. "Don't take me back to Tenn Galon," she breathed in my ear. "He'll kill me." She squeezed the growing interest in between my legs, her body hot and inviting, like her parted lips. "We can be together—knock off Bim and take over his operation!"

She was a woman, all right: scheming and manipulative, and very, very restless.

I clipped her on the chin again, the bruise I raised there branding her as off-limits.

All I wanted to do was deliver unto Tenn Galon what was his. And then get the hell off that wild desert planet where the waters ran too deep for the likes of me to fathom.

✗

PENNWOOD AVENUE

Sanford Zane Meschkow

There was no getting around it; the basement laundry sink needed scrubbing out. The two-story brick house Jake Weaver had inherited from his parents needed maintenance and the work helped him put his time in Vietnam behind him. Even waxing the floors and cutting the front and back lawn was better than brooding. Someday he would marry and start a family in this house. He didn't dare let it start to crumble. After he ate breakfast and fed White Rabbit, he collected what he needed and got busy. It was a mystery to him how all that foamy water could somehow get that sink so dirty.

The phone in the living room rang. And kept on ringing. There he was with gloves foamy with cleanser and, of course, no phone in the basement. He said a few Vietnamese words not found in most phrase books, peeled off one of his gloves and trudged up the stairs as the phone rang on. He had an idea it might be Shaky Stan.

"Jacob?" Then silence and no garage noises in the background.

"Yeah, it's Jake, Stan. Hey, what's up? Shouldn't you be at the garage?"

Damn, he was holding the phone with the hand with the glove on. What a slimy mess.

"I called in sick today. I had a bad night last night. Can we get together for lunch today? I really need to talk."

Jake looked at the clock on the mantle. "Had your breakfast yet? I bet not. Okay, we'll have brunch. I'll be right down. What's wrong?"

"Old Rose is gone. Her family showed up last night and just dragged her out of the building to put her in some kind of retirement home. She was screaming as they carried her down the stairs. Her balls of wool are all over the stairs, her apartment door is open and kids are coming in and *stealing* stuff." Stan sounded like he was crying.

"Okay. Don't try and do anything about it. Don't go out; just lock your door. I'll be down there in less than an hour."

Rose's family had been neglecting her, so Stan had been shopping and cooking for her. Now Stan was the only white tenant on his block in a North Philadelphia neighborhood that had become a drug bazaar. It was time to get him out of there.

Mmmrruupp? White Rabbit rubbed against his legs. She was a fixed female cat with orange fur and golden eyes. A real lady and too polite to hop into bed with him. She would rather sit in the chair across the room from his bed and guard him as he slept. Somehow she kept the bad dreams about Tet away. No bright flashes, no bodies flying through the air. Just sleep.

"Hey, babe, how would you like to have Stan living with us for a while?"

✗   ✗   ✗   ✗

Stan said no to Jake taking them to Philadelphia's Chinatown for a great Chinese meal, so they just ate bad local take-out Chinese in Stan's tiny kitchen. As they parked in front of Stan's place, they had passed a few guys helping themselves to the furniture from Old Rose's apartment. Jake didn't like the way they checked out his car. After all, he had suburban plates; they might try to sell him drugs. He hoped on their next trip they would trip over Old Rose's stuff on the stairs and break some bones.

Stan was calmer with some food in him and having Jake to talk with. Now was the time to talk some sense into him.

"Stan, why are you living here? You're a really good auto mechanic. Can't you see this block is becoming the Wild West? Doesn't the noise of the kids driving in from the suburbs looking for drug buys every night keep you awake?"

"It's close to Dad's garage. And I don't make that much. The garage has to support my uncle's family and my two brother's families besides me."

"Well, maybe there would be more money to go around if you worked elsewhere. And you would make more if you worked near I live. And you wouldn't have to live in a roach ranch like this, either."

"Come on, Jake. A garage that works on Jags isn't going to hire me."

"Hey, we have garages for working people, too. Not everybody on the Main Line is a millionaire. On my street in Wynnewood there are teachers, salesmen, small business owners. The big money lives miles farther out of town."

"But the rents out there would kill me."

"Not if you move in with me and White Rabbit. Stay a year if you want. But I'll have to throw you out if I start dating. Hey, maybe we'll double date? Come on, think about it."

Yeah, it would be nice to take a date someplace the Viet Cong won't blow up, thought Jake.

Jake looked around Stan's kitchen and peered into his half-empty refrigerator. Jake checked the clock. Almost noon. The human tigers and wolves in this neighborhood were probably still asleep. It should be safe to walk around the block to the supermarket. Jake didn't want to lose his parking spot just in case he could convince Stan to pack a few suitcases and move to Pennwood Avenue tonight. Then White Rabbit could drive the bad dreams away from both of them.

By the time they had walked around the corner Stan was already thinking of reasons not to move. Jake saw nobody on the street but women with kids and a few old folks.

"Yeah, it's a bad neighborhood, but just wait until Frank Rizzo wins the race for mayor. He'll get tough with the drug dealers around here and the good people will get their neighborhood back."

"Sure, Stan. And is supercop Rizzo going to reopen a few of those abandoned factories around here so those drug dealers can find jobs?"

"Hey, there's no law that says you can't leave Philadelphia and go find work. Our families left Europe on steamships and they did fine. All these kids have to do is save a few bucks and buy a bus ticket."

"Yeah. There are lots of jobs for black cowboys in Wyoming, especially any who've never ridden a horse."

Down the street they went arguing and Jake was suddenly happier than he had been in a long time, because Stan was arguing back, just like in the old days in Pittman's Camp Southpaw where, besides all the booze, grass and girl chasing, you could get into all-night arguments about the craziest subjects. Were flying saucers actually real or not? Could Hitler have somehow have won WWII? Would Soviet Russia and Red China ever fight a war with each other? It had been the happiest time of his life.

Stan was speaking, but Jake had stopped listening. His off-duty Saigon street sense was suddenly waking up. There were three young blacks with Afros and sunglasses coming out on the porch of one of the houses they were about to pass. One was carrying a briefcase. Two white men in suits too nice for the neighborhood were stepping out of a black 1971 Cadillac sedan in front of the house and one of them also had a briefcase.

Then the three young blacks turned to look at Stan and Jake and their faces began to register surprise and the white man who wasn't carrying the briefcase also began to turn toward them and began to reach into his jacket and his face began to change as well. *Oh, no, the VC are in town today.*

"*Down!*" Jake yelled and pulled Stan off the sidewalk and into the space in the street between a dusty Ford with flat tires and a rusty Volkswagen bus. Bullets smashed through the windows of the bus and shards of glass rained down on them. Jake never heard those shots. But he did hear the BOOM! BOOM! of a shotgun going off and then lots of cursing and screaming. Then there were some shots from a handgun, then silence, except for the shouting of other people on the street. Jake fully expected someone to walk around the corner of the Volkswagen and put a bullet in his face, but nothing happened.

"Stay on the ground, Stan. We're crawling over to my car and getting out of here." Then, without looking back, he started crawling up the street back the way they had come, the hot pavement almost blistering his hands. He crawled away from one scene of disaster before in real life and many times more in nightmares, so it was if he had been rehearsing for today. He hoped Stan was keeping up with him.

He was. Jake pulled Stan to his feet as they reached the corner. "Walk slowly back to my car. Keep your head down, but don't run."

"Jake, what do you think happened back there?" To his credit, Stan didn't sound as shaky as Jake had expected. Jake was fighting the urge to collapse and just shiver.

"I think we walked into the middle of a drug deal and maybe one party thought we were cops and the other guys thought we were working for the other gang. Stan, get in your car and follow me over to my house. You're moving in with me right now whether you want to or not."

"But don't we want to stick around to talk to the cops?"

"Not in this neighborhood, I wouldn't. Do your want to give your name and address? Suppose by the time the cops get here either the cash or the drugs are nowhere to be found? And, no, we are not going to stop for you to get your PJs or a toothbrush. As far as I'm concerned, this is now Viet Cong country now."

✗ ✗ ✗ ✗

They called it "shell shock" in WWI, "battle fatigue" in WWII. There was probably a new name for it now, like "Vietnam depression syndrome". Guys who were scared about being sent to Vietnam could always flee to Canada. But where could guys who came home from Vietnam with depression flee?

The only way Jake had learned to survive his depression was by pretending he was some being dropped off by a flying saucer who had to pass for human. So every day

He had to go through the motions: get up, use the bathroom, shave, get dressed, make breakfast and so on and so on for all his days and months and years. It was that or else he would collapse on his bed and doze for 18 or 20 hours a day.

What was helpful was the need to help Stan move out of his apartment, move into his house, go shopping with him for food and other tasks until the morning Stan drove off to do a valve job at his father's garage.

After breakfast Jake thought about doing the sink, but then looked out the front door and noticed that the grass looked high. He could do the sink later.

He was getting ready to go out to the garage when the doorbell rang. There was a red Corvette parked out front and a nice-looking redhead with green eyes was at the door. She was carrying a briefcase and was dressed in a blue business suit with a pearl necklace and pearl earrings. Even if she was selling cemetery plots he was definitely going to speak with her.

"Good morning. Is this 330 Pennwood Avenue? And do you own this property?"

"Yes, that's the right address and I'm the owner. Call me Jake."

"Jake, I'm Samantha Harwood, Harwood Realty. I would like to take a few minutes of your time and discuss the money you could make putting your property up for sale with us." She handed him a business card. Even her hand was beautiful.

Sell his home? Inconceivable. But the grass could wait.

"You said the magic word. Living room is to the right." As he stepped aside for her he noted her legs and the rest of her. Nice scenery.

"I saw the contactor's truck in the driveway. Is that you?"

"My father started the business. I'm the 'and Son'"

"And if I may ask, who does your landscaping? Your yard looks wonderful."

"Actually, I do."

She looked around the living room as she sat down. She couldn't miss seeing the South Vietnamese flag over the mantelpiece, but said nothing about it.

"I sense a very well-maintained house that will show well and sell for a nice price. You know, Jake, lots of people would like to sell, but they can't face the uphill battle of getting their house in shape for sale. But that wouldn't be a problem for you. You're not married, are you? No kids?"

"No."

"Well, if you were you would know that you are in one of the finest school systems in Pennsylvania and within walking distance of a great elementary school. A young couple who want to raise their kids out of the city would jump at the chance to buy this house."

"It's got a small back yard. And a garage that is more like a tool shed."

"Yes, it's a starter house. I bet your parents moved in right after WWII, right? Do you know what you could sell it for now? Here's the price range you might get. I'll be able to name a better figure if you show me around the place." She handed him a typed page that seemed have been copied from his township tax assessment. The top of the price range was amazing.

She stood up, eyes sparkling. "You didn't make your bed this morning, Jake? Who cares? Come on, I've seen houses rented to college students that looked like the morning after a cattle stampede. Let's start with the basement."

So, basement, eat-in kitchen, living room, master bedroom, the bedroom that he had turned into his contracting business office and then a quick peek at the room where Stan was staying. She peered into closets, the bathroom and even climbed up to take a fast peek at the attic and asked about how old the roof was. She wanted to see the garage, too. She was so full of energy. His book collection interested her.

"Jake, how many bookshelves do you have in this house? There seems to be one in every room."

"I think eight. I wasn't very good in school. I needed to read things and think them over. I guess I was the kid in the neighborhood who everyone gave their old books to. On these shelves I have almost every book Mark Twain wrote."

He reached out to a shelf and pulled out a fat volume.

"Hey, here's one of the four volumes of *The World of Mathematics*. I was terrible in math and my math teacher and I hated each other. I thought these books would help my marks. Well, they didn't, but I learned math is such amazing stuff. This chapter is about Srinivasa Ramanujan, a clerk from India who was a mathematical genius who independently recreated about 100 years of Western mathematics based on an old math book and derived functions that modern mathematicians still don't know how he proved. He reminds me of Leonardo da Vinci dreaming of building flying machines with nobody to help him. That's sad." There was a long silence. Jake was suddenly aware of how close together they were in the dark hallway. She smelled like lilacs.

"Jake," she said softly, "You sound like a grownup who should go back to school again. Hey, you wouldn't happen to have any coffee in the house, would you?"

They ended up at the kitchen table. There was coffee in the pot and although it wasn't hot she insisted on drinking it. "As long as it's brown and has caffeine in it, I'll drink it," she said with a laugh.

"Jake, I'm not here to push you. Stick my card somewhere and think about it. And thanks for being such a good sport. Most people don't let me look at their attic."

They shook hands at the front door. His cat came over to say "so long".

"What a lovely cat. Has it a name?"

"White Rabbit."

"A Grace Slick fan, I presume?"

"Yeah, since forever." He didn't mean to sound so lonely, but it slipped out.

She grabbed his hand again. "Look, even if you don't sell, I hear from someone big in real estate that a lot of people will leave Philadelphia after Frank Rizzo becomes the mayor. Lots of houses around here will change hands and new owners will need a good contractor. So keep your contracting business going, okay?"

He sat on the stairs after she drove off and White Rabbit jumped into his lap to keep him company. He hadn't had the guts to even ask for a coffee date. He might need her company, but he didn't want to beg for it. No, but actually he almost had.

If he didn't get his life back soon he might become an old man in a dirty bathrobe. He felt good helping Stan. Maybe having Stan around would help him get his life back as well. Perhaps.

✗ ✗ ✗ ✗

In the next few days he convinced Stan's family to let him try to help Stan find a job elsewhere and got Stan started on making the rounds of suburban garages.

The morning Stan started job hunting, Jake saw that the grass in the front lawn was really shooting up; he couldn't stand it. He got the lawnmower out of the garage and started cutting. He was almost done when a black 1971 Cadillac sedan pulled up to the curb and a big guy got out from the driver's side and an even bigger guy got out of the other side. Big Guy shut off the lawnmower. Bigger Guy shoved something hard into his ribs. "You're late for a meeting, pal," he said. Something about the car and the suits looked familiar. Oh, boy, it was Viet Cong time again, this time a mile west of the city line. He was shocked.

Bigger put an arm lock on him and marched him to the back seat of the Cadillac. Big climbed in the front seat and pointed a snub-nosed .38 revolver at him while Bigger tied his hands behind his back and blindfolded him.

It was a long and quiet drive. The car smelled new. Jake was tired enough from cutting the lawn that he was actually about to doze off when the car made a series of sharp turns and stopped. Bigger pulled the blindfold off, dropped it on the back seat and shoved Jake out of the car, up a broad stone stairway and through a gigantic wooden door. He was being pushed into a huge stone mansion that resembled a castle.

Inside the door was an empty kitchen full of delicious smells. The two thugs shoved him through the kitchen and then down a hall past a room where a few more thugs seemed to be playing cards, laughing and joking and having a great time. Two or three more shoves down the hall got him into a big room with tall French doors that looked out on a terrace. It had once been a library and hundreds of books were still there, but now half of it was a monster of an office.

Across the room were some filing cabinets and a black woman with an astounding figure pounding away on a Selectric. Most of the floor space in front of the French doors was taken up with a huge antique table with piles of ledgers and file folders, telephones and other office stuff. Behind the table sat a bear-like red-bearded man in what had to be the most expensive suit Jake had ever seen.

He waved at Big and Bigger and pointed at the middle of the three throne-like antique chairs across the table from him. "Untie him and sit him down, guys and then go get some lunch." He sounded very cheerful. From somewhere one of the two thugs produced a very sharp knife and cut through the rope around his wrists. Jake felt loops of rope drop off and a normal amount of blood racing into his hands again. It hurt.

He decided to make believe it didn't. Jake tried to glare at Red Beard but it was a waste of time. The big guy just stared back at him, faintly amused.

"So, you're Jake the Contractor," he said. "Watch him, Leon."

Sitting in the chair to the left of him was another thug with bushy eyebrows, but this one looked angry enough to tear him apart. And huddled deep into the chair to his right was…Samantha. She didn't seem to want to look at him, but kept her gaze fixed on the guy who had to be her boss. Jake turned back to Red Beard and said nothing.

"I'm sure you have questions, Jake, but you don't seem to want to ask them, so I'll answer them for you. First, in addition to her great body, is Denise an adequate secretary for my needs? Oh, yes, good at dictation and typing and filing. But then a lot of my business does not ever involve written records." He raised his voice. "Oh, Denise, honey, why don't you take a break for a half hour or so?" He chuckled as Denise fled the room as if terrified.

"I think your second question might be is Samantha an actual real estate agent? No, not really, but I do have real estate interests, especially in the neighborhood where your friend Stan used to live. In fact, you did me a small favor getting him out of there. People who work for me want to use that building for something else. Actually, what Samantha contributes to my organization is her ability to find all the information I might need about people. Still no questions?"

Jake wondered if Red Beard had anything to do with the sudden decision of Old Rose's family to pull her out of the building so abruptly. Probably yes, but he decided to ignore that opening.

"So, what did she tell you about me?" asked Jake.

"Well, your contracting business earns you peanuts. You've lost most of your father's old customers. Your parents invested in some stocks over the years and you get some dividend checks now and then. But your big income provider is a company in Los Angeles owned by some Vietnamese refugee families that have some strip mall properties. You must be a silent partner because those checks are big. It makes one wonder if maybe that company does some other kind of business. Like dealing dope?"

"No. Those people are clean. My background is in intelligence in Vietnam. They ratted on some colleagues who were helping the Viet Cong, so they had to get out of the country. Some friends and I passed the hat to help them. They promised to pay us back and more. I'm the only one who helped them still alive, so they are sending me all the money now. That's why I haven't lost my parent's house."

"That's a great story. It's right out of *Steve Canyon*. So what were you doing walking around in my neighborhood and disrupting my business? Leon says his friend Rex made you as a cop and so did a bunch of my people who saw you on my street. I saw the way you looked this room over when you were pushed into it. I smell a narc, Jake."

Samantha raised her hand. "Boss, if I may add something here?"

"Go ahead."

"Have you ever considered that Jake's walking into the middle of a drug deal in broad daylight was a complete accident? Also, his house is full of books. Maybe he's just *smart*."

"Oh, I see. A contractor who reads girlie magazines for the interviews. Well, let's see. Leon, go over to the shelves there and pull me out a book. How about one of those big green ones? All great American novels, I think. Give one to Jake." Red Beard watched Leon drop the book into Jake's lap.

"It's *The Last of the Mohicans*, boss."

"Great. Okay, Jake, tell me all about the book."

It took Jake a long moment before he could speak. He took a deep breath

"Well, Cooper may be a fine storyteller, but he's a terrible writer. Hawk-eye talks like a backwoodsman in one paragraph and is almost sprouting poetry like an Oxford graduate a few paragraphs later. Cooper has Indians doing totally dumb things like jumping out of a tree down to a flatboat float-ing down a river one by one and all landing in the water. There's a scene in the fog where Hawkeye and the commander of the fort's two daughters are lost and can't find the fort, so the fort starts firing cannons to lead them to safety and this cannon ball just rolls out of the fog right in front of them. Who in his right mind would fire loaded cannons that might hit his commanding officer's daughters? They are going to need those cannon balls when the French attack, so—"

Samantha reached over and put her hand over Jake's mouth. "That's enough, Jake. I can tell you're starting to bore him. There's another point, boss. Haven't you heard that a lot of people are going to vote for Frank Rizzo because they think he will really crack down on crime? It's in the papers. Why would a bunch of smart Orientals want to move into your territory if Rizzo's going to win?"

Red Beard chuckled. "Well, I'm not afraid of Rizzo. I don't care if Saint Peter becomes mayor. There will always be cops who will take money and look the other way." He pointed to Jake. "You! I have pictures of you shop-ping with your pal. I'm handing them out to my people. If anyone ever sees you in my part of town I'll send Leon out to get you both, understand me? And I have friends who are bankers. They'll watch your account. If your Vietnamese pals start shipping huge bundles of cash into your account you'll be in big trouble. Samantha, drive this guy home and on the way tell him how smart it would be to never mention this meeting. And take the evening off. Denise is getting tired of seeing your skinny ass around here."

Leon's face turned very red. "Hey, Boss, he got Rex shot. He's supposed to be mine."

"You've got more important things to do, Leon, like holding a meeting with the guys starting now about how to avoid future accidents. Perhaps you should watch some old gangster movies and see how they do it. Okay, meeting's over. Hey, Denise! Get your great bod in here!" He seemed very pleased with himself.

Samantha grabbed Jake by the hand and pulled him out of his chair and down the hall. The stress had exhausted him so much that he could barely walk.

"What wrong? Are you going to be sick? Don't fall down because I'm sure Leon will just walk over here and start kicking you."

"I'm kind of stressed out. Who is Rex? Did he and Leon go to Princeton together or something?"

"They were very, very, um, close."

"Oh. I thought gangsters didn't tolerate that sort of thing."

"The boss doesn't care. He just uses that to needle Leon just like he needles everybody. Hey, I notice you don't seem to be too angry with me. Why not?"

"Because maybe you just saved my life in there. Why? Does this place need a new water heater or something? I'll give you a good price."

"Very funny. You're a riot. Talk in the car. Boy, could you use a shower." Samantha's red Corvette was at the end of a long line of shiny Cadillacs.

"My orders are to blindfold you again. Sorry," she said.

"I'll probably spent most of the ride with my eyes closed and shaking all over anyway."

But he got a good enough look around to recognize where he was. Newtown Township, which was west of Philadelphia. Lots of horse farms, mansions and country clubs. He could find this place again. And he wanted to.

"Jake, is Cooper's book really that bad? I've never read it."

"Me neither. But I remembered Mark Twain's review of it and swiped a lot from it. I guess I passed the test."

"The Boss is too smart…Don't try that again, okay?"

After a few miles, Samantha parked the car and took the blindfold off.

"Okay. I want you to reach under the dashboard in front of you and feel around for an envelope taped back there."

The tiny envelope was brown and inside it was a photostat of an ID card with Samantha's picture on it. He closed the envelope instantly.

"Holy cow, you're some kind of Federal cop. How did you get into Red Beard's organization? Why show me this?"

"That's none of your business. It didn't involve a casting couch, if you want to know. Denise takes care of that part of the operation for him. But I must ask you some questions. What is Camp Southpaw and what did you do there?"

"I can't answer that. It might be still operational. Why are you even asking?"

"Because when I tried to check your Army records I found they were locked in a big vault somewhere. You were a very spooky somebody. Is doing plumbing jobs just your cover? Is Army Intelligence also after this monster? I saw him first. Damn, I want to put the cuffs on him myself. And his whole operation, if possible."

"Be my guest. I'm no longer an active agent. Battle fatigue. Our whole section was in a restaurant for a wedding reception during Tet and the Viet Cong blew it up. Just a coincidence? I don't know. My pal Stan and I used to work in the same section, and we were the only two we know of who got out alive. At least he's recovered enough to hold down a job with a little handholding. I may never shake this. I may end up in a VA hospital someday weaving baskets."

"Not if I can help it." She didn't say it; she growled it. "So why are there no Army pension checks in your bank records?"

"It's complicated. We were sort of off the books and some of the people who could provide the paperwork I would need died in the blast. I also think some people want to forget all about Camp Southpaw. Besides, I'm not an officer. On the books I'm still a corporal. How much could I get?"

"Okay. My advice is don't tell anyone about this afternoon. Leon likes shooting people, so don't tempt him. I'll sniff around and see if I can get you some additional money."

"So you plan to ride to my rescue."

"You and White Rabbit. We Jefferson Airplane fans have to stick together."

"Thanks. And I don't think you have a skinny ass. In fact, I think you are magnificent all over."

"Yeah, I could tell. You almost had me there telling me stories about poor Srinivasa Ramanujan. I had to look him up."

"Your boss is testing us, isn't he? What if you turned up in a few hours with a bag full of silverware? You could say I asked you in for coffee and made a grab for you and you hit me with a vase. Then you swiped the family silverware as you left the house. That would prove to him we're not friends. I bet that would help you and he would really enjoy hearing that."

"And I wrote 'So long, sucker!' in lipstick on your bathroom mirror? Yeah, but I would rather you saved your silverware for a romantic candlelight dinner on a night I can't stand to eat dinner again with a murderous lunatic. But not this week. A spy has to work two jobs, you know." She reached out and took his hand. "But, Jake, I know where you live. Just don't leave town, okay? And *don't* dare try to rescue me."

"Yes, Your Majesty."

They drove all the back to Pennwood Avenue holding hands.

And the next day Stan landed a new job and Jake got to scrub out the basement sink.

✗

Sanford Zane Meschkow is a retired technical writer and editor with one published science fiction story to his credit who is nostalgic about the early 1970s when he first came to Philadelphia. "There was a drug bazaar neighborhood in North Philadelphia and Frank Rizzo was a strong law-and-order candidate for mayor running in the summer of 1971," he says. "In the next Jake and Stan story, reaction to the news of Nixon's upcoming visit to China sets up the situation for Jake's next brush with criminals." Fans of rock music might notice the absence of popular tunes of the day. "I'm not a Vietnam vet, but I have suffered from depression. Jake's house is silent because I couldn't bear to hear rock music when I was depressed. But I promise to bring Samantha back into Jake's life, but all in good time!"

ABOVE SUSPICION

Victoria Weisfeld

Boston, Conley Terminal, Sunday, March 18, 1990

Shortly before 9 a.m., Amit Madoor and his nephew Rashid arrived at the Port of Boston's Conley Terminal in two vintage Cadillacs. Dockhands directed them to park in a cavernous prep bay, where they emptied the cars's gasoline tanks and disconnected their batteries. A tow-truck maneuvered the two beauties into the open mouth of a steel shipping container and the workers clambered in behind to pack protective padding around and between them. End-to-end, the Caddies just about filled the forty-foot box.

Before the container was sealed, every dockworker having a spare minute strolled over to admire these cars—classics from 1956 and 1959—one purple and the other two-tone, turquoise and white. They peered through the windows at the immaculate leather upholstery, ran their hands over the fins and admired the wide whitewall tires. If circumstances allowed, they would have popped the hoods to check out the 325-horsepower engines. Drifting back to their work, they slapped each other on the back, recalling the hand-me-down cars of their youth. Every man of them would fantasize about these gleaming chariots, but they embodied no man's dreams more than Amit Madoor's.

✗ ✗ ✗ ✗

As soon as the container door clanged shut, Rashid said, "Gotta go. Noon clinic."

They embraced, the younger man kissing his uncle on both cheeks.

Madoor reached inside his suit jacket and pulled out his wallet. "Here. Please. Take some dollars for a taxicab."

"No. Thanks." Rashid pushed the bills away. "I'll jog partway, then catch the T to the hospital."

"Take a cab." Madoor nudged the money toward him, but Rashid ignored it.

"Uncle Amit, it was great to see you." Rashid reached out to shake his uncle's hand. Rashid was still in medical training, while Madoor, despite the closeness in their ages, wore his businessman's responsibilities like an extra overcoat.

"Thank you for your help," he said. "I will be always in your debt."

"Travel safely and maybe I'll visit you in Rome when my residency is finally over."

"I hope that you will. Be well."

Rashid jogged away, returning to his world of lecture halls and laboratories, the dwindling ill and the kinetic young doctors. When he was out of sight, Madoor turned back to the dock. His container, inspected and sealed, awaited pickup. The word "Evergreen" stenciled on its side seemed auspicious to him, a Muslim man.

He stood just inside the doorway of a low building and watched until the tall post-Panamax crane winched his container into the air, swung it into position and settled it on one of the rising stacks of red, yellow, green and blue containers like rust-streaked Lego bricks. None of the longshoremen were near enough to see his gloved hands clenching and unclenching or hear his long exhale once the container was safely aboard ship. Now it rested, hidden in plain sight among hundreds of others already loaded onto the *Annamarie*, scheduled for departure at noon Tuesday for the free port of Trieste.

He turned from the dock and walked toward the exit. Sirens in the distance slowed his steps, but when their shrill screams faded, he hurried on his way.

Boston, Sunday, February 18, 1990

A month before their early morning on the docks, Madoor and his nephew walked along the snowy strip of parkland bordering the Charles River Basin. A few puffing joggers and a well-bundled dog walker were the only other people braving the snow-streaked path. Even so, they kept their voices low and said little more than necessary.

"You asked me to find two physician residents who are—what word did you use? daring?" Rashid said. "I have them! Real cowboys. Technically, they're good surgeons, but they have that extra dose of confidence, that 'I can do anything' arrogance surgical specialists are prone to."

"If a doctor is planning to cut into me, I do not want him to have doubts!"

"As long as he's right."

"Yes. As you say, technically skilled."

"I don't know—don't need to know—why you want them, but these two are special. They do high-risk procedures all day, every day. As our residency director says, 'nerves of steel.'"

"A valuable trait. But would they be willing to help a stranger? All I can offer them is money." Madoor studied the ice clogging the river, willing one particular piece to break free. Rid of this one obstacle, the rest of the ice would flow freely to Boston Harbor, just as finding the right doctors would put his plans in motion.

"That's the other thing. They're totally obsessed about the state of their finances. That's not unusual. Most doctors leaving training worry about their debt. But these two never stop talking about it."

"How well do they know you? I don't want them to suspect our connection."

"They're a couple years ahead of me, so I'm invisible to them. Plus, I'm in general medicine, not surgery."

"Do they get along? Or are they competitors?" He watched the chunk of ice jostle its neighbors, slip past them and begin to move swiftly in the current.

"Actually, they're in different specialties. One's a neurosurgeon—"

"Neuro—?"

"Brain," Rashid said, "—and the other, orthopedics. Bones. And they're friends."

Madoor removed a glove to reach into his trouser pocket and pull out something small. He took Rashid's hand and closed it around the object.

"What's this?" Rashid asked, opening his gloved palm. On the black leather shone a platinum ring set with a carved crystal.

"For you. Your grandfather wants you to have it."

"Wow." Rashid held the ring up sideways, allowing sunlight to pass through the dome of the crystal. "It's beautiful."

"He is very proud of you. As am I. You will do great things, Rashid."

"Thank you, Uncle. He's been generous to us both. Paying my medical tuition. Helping you buy your shop."

"If we were not already determined to be successful, we would want to make something of ourselves just for him." Madoor paused. "He is dying, you know."

"The cancer is back?"

"Yes, your grandmother says he will be gone before summer. Which is why he is doing these last things for us, these last gifts." He gestured to the ring in Rashid's hand.

"We should bring him here." Rashid swung around to gaze at the looming Massachusetts General Hospital complex, as if a miracle lay waiting behind those stone and glass facades.

"You know he will not leave Fez. He is at peace there, surrounded by people who love him."

Rashid swallowed hard, a time or two. "He has helped so many."

"Yes, he has." Madoor didn't mention the extra generosity his father recently extended to him—partly in the form of a loan and partly in something even more valuable, contacts—or the heavy obligation he felt to use them well.

Wednesday, February 28, 1990, noon

"What would you do if you had a million dollars?" Madoor asked the two surgical residents. They agreed to a quick lunch of sandwiches and coffee in a bustling Fruit Street diner hard by Massachusetts General Hospital on the strength of a "business proposition" Madoor said he hoped to tell them about.

He came to their meeting wearing a three-piece charcoal wool suit with a precisely knotted silver-grey tie and shoes shined that morning, whereas they wore wrinkled green cotton scrubs too thin for the weather and open-backed clogs. He'd folded his overcoat over an empty chair and his hat occupied the seat. The knitted sleeve-ends of the doctors's slippery down jackets thrown onto the backs of their chairs now trailed in dirty puddles of slush.

They looked run ragged, especially Jack, the neurosurgeon-in-training. Isaac, the orthopedics resident, was taller, younger and less intense. By lunchtime, they said, they'd been on their feet six hours already and they described some of the intricate repairs made to the brains and bones of their patients. They put in this level of effort, even though emergency cases kept them at the hospital until nearly one a.m. the night before.

"A million dollars!" The residents said together and burst out laughing. People at neighboring tables glanced over, including Madoor's nephew Rashid. The two surgeons, confident they knew everything important that was relevant to their lives, did not know about Madoor's relationship to one of their fellow trainees, nor that Rashid hand-picked them from the hospital's white-coated flock and told his uncle how to contact them.

"I am serious," Madoor said. His smile was sufficient to show good humor, crinkling the skin around his black eyes, but not enough to suggest he might be joking.

They regarded him closely, jutting out their chins and narrowing their gaze, as if trying to establish a diagnosis, though Madoor already observed much more about them than they would ever learn about him. Jack leaned far back in his chair and drummed the table a few times with the flat of his hands. Quietly now, he said, "Christ, Isaac, I think maybe he is."

"In my dreams," Isaac said and took another bite of a tuna on rye.

Jack leaned across his half-eaten sandwich. "I can tell you what I'd do with a million. I'd pay off my medical school loans and be a free man—free to start my own practice, free to move to San Diego. I'd dump that piece-of-shit hatchback, get a decent car and tool around Southern California with the top down. Man, I'd be set. Instead of a long slog trying to stay ahead of the debt-collector." He turned to his friend. "You?"

"I'd buy a really great apartment back home in Florida. Miami Beach. I'm thirty years old, for Chrissake. My fiancée and I want to get married, but she's not moving up here, that's for damn sure." He glanced out the window at the snow, coming down harder now, obscuring the dirty slush and treacherous patches of sidewalk ice.

"Thirty? I'm almost thirty-five and I don't even have a girlfriend," Jack said.

"What happened to—"

"She broke up with me. Said I never had time for her. Which is true." He pulled a disgusted face. "And my career's not even started. I won't dig out from under for years, while you're down in Miami rebuilding the hips and shoulders of all those old farts."

"The possibility interests you then?" Madoor said.

"The possibility interests me like winning the lottery interests me," Jack said, keeping his voice low. "But it ain't happening. Isaac's family, they could stake him, but not mine."

"But they won't." Isaac turned to Madoor. "My family thinks I'll make millions as an orthopedic surgeon and maybe someday I will. But I need money to get started." He pushed his empty plate away.

"You could have it." Madoor smiled. "I will gladly tell you how. But only if you have the nerve to go after it. Not everyone would. Please think how much easier your lives could be."

"For doing what, exactly?" Isaac asked.

Madoor shook his head. "When I tell you, it won't sound as dramatic or as worrisome as whatever you are thinking right now. It will be—easy. But first I must be sure that you are willing."

The waitress brought the check and Madoor reached for it. He opened his wallet and gave each of them a card from the Copley Plaza, his room number written on the back.

"Thank you for your time. I know my request to meet you was uncomfortably vague. And still is. But it will not be for long, depending on you."

"Hey, we had to eat," Jack said. He stirred his coffee.

"Good afternoon, gentlemen. I hope we meet again." Madoor walked to the cash register, pulling on his coat and positioning the trilby over his black hair. He shoved a tip in the jar and walked out into the snowstorm.

Boston, Early March, 1990

In the following days, while Madoor waited to see whether the residents would take the bait, he walked the city, including its rundown industrial areas. He explored streets with small workshops, listening for noisy hammering and the whine of band saws, following the smell of motor oil and hot metal that flowed out when the rolling doors rattled up. He was in search of a special kind of neighborhood, one like those of his Moroccan childhood and someone with particular skills.

Evenings he stayed in his hotel room, ordered room-service dinners and chuckled over his reading of Salman Rushdie's *The Satanic Verses*. He was more than a hundred pages in when the phone rang. The surgeons wanted to talk again. Madoor suggested they meet in the Public Garden near the "Make Way for Ducklings" sculpture, the line of eight bronze ducklings trailing their mother at the edge of the park lawn.

At the appointed time the next day, a Saturday, they found a bench to share and Madoor described what they would have to do. He studied their reactions as they grasped the implications of his plan and for a few moments he thought it possible he would lose them. But his logic was persuasive. The job was simple. It entailed no violence. Everything was worked out. They just needed to follow the steps.

It would require two hours of their time at most, after which they could resume their normal lives, lives that would be so much easier with a million dollars apiece in special bank accounts, about which questions would never be raised. He stopped talking and let them think. From their body language, he was soon convinced they were talking themselves into it. Jack first.

"You know," Jack said, "most people don't have any idea about the huge amount of debt we end up with—from medical school and then from the low salaries we get as residents. Boston is expensive. And we're not living like kings, I assure you."

His friend snorted and Madoor nodded thoughtfully.

"Then we have to decide whether to go into practice by ourselves—and that costs a bundle—real estate, hiring people, equipment, getting set up, malpractice insurance, marketing—or join some existing practice. In my specialty—Isaac's, too—we're probably better off going in with someone. But it's a gamble how that relationship will work out."

Madoor watched a couple of determined pigeons trail a child eating a cookie.

"We'll be the low men on the totem-pole for a few *more* years. Medicaid patients, on-call," Jack said.

Madoor had no idea what he was talking about, but nodded again.

"But if we went into an existing practice with something in our hand— you know, technology they don't typically have—*plus* the experience using it, then we could negotiate."

"Get a *much* better deal," Isaac said.

"We have the most spectacular technology right here. If we could offer to replicate a piece of it, we'd be really value-add."

They thought a few minutes longer. Finally Jack stretched his arms across the back of the bench and squinted up into the wan spring sunshine filtering through the trees'sstill-bare branches. "We can do this."

"Well, sure we *can*." Isaac's emphasis was an unspoken "But should we?"

"Isaac, c'mon, man. It's a fucking gift from God." Jack slapped the bench. "I've put my life on hold long enough. San Diego, dude!"

Isaac leaned over staring at his dirty boots.

A mother and her bundled-up twins wove in and out among the duck-lings, laughing. The children ran past the bench where the men sat, splashing muddy slush onto Isaac, even getting some in his hair.

He brushed off the wet stuff and turned to Jack, grinning. "A great *big* gift from God." He was in.

A quote from Rushdie came to Madoor. It was about how men use God to justify the unjustifiable. And how so often, as in the present case, God has nothing whatever to do with it. He kept this thought to himself.

Now that the surgeons agreed to perform the job, Madoor set his hook with various assurances and payment details. They didn't waver. In their minds, he thought, the money was already spent.

Sunday, March 18, 11 a.m.

On the morning that Madoor watched the steel containers being loaded onto the *Annamarie's* deck, dazed officials of the Isabella Stewart Gardner Museum wandered its Italianate galleries clutching clipboards and mumbling to Boston police detectives. FBI investigators were on their way and the media frenzy over the largest property theft in history was about to explode.

"So what's missing?" Detective Morris Kahn asked the curator stumbling along beside him. "We've been all over this place."

She checked the list recorded in her shaky handwriting and ticked off the losses. Five paintings: one of only about thirty-five known Vermeers, two Rembrandts, a Manet, a Flinck. Works on paper: a Rembrandt self-portrait the size of a postage stamp and five Degas drawings, three featuring horses. A three-thousand-year-old Chinese bronze beaker and, oddest of all, an eagle-shaped finial snatched from atop a Napoleonic banner. She swallowed hard. "It looks like they couldn't pry the banner frame itself off the wall.... Too many screws." Her voice disappeared into a whisper.

"What's the value of all this?"

She brushed at her eyes. "Priceless."

Kahn and his detectives pieced together the story of the theft from the physical evidence, the hard drive of the motion detector equipment and their interviews with the guards. The long and the short of it was while Boston's St. Patrick's Day celebrations wound down, a pair of men dressed in the dark blue uniforms and service caps of city police officers gained entry to the museum's side entrance on Palace Road. More experienced—and alert— museum personnel might have asked them a few questions or followed the written security policy, which forbade unlocking the doors for any unknown person, but Kahn kept this opinion to himself. Second-guessing now was salt in the wound.

The detectives interviewed the two night guards separately. The twenty-three-year-old who unlocked the security doors wore his curly hair past his shoulders and Kahn's two neatly groomed younger detectives rolled their eyes as he explained how he'd been on edge.

"First a fire alarm went off upstairs. I checked it out—nothing, except the strobe lights flashing like maniacs. Then—and this shit never happens here—an alarm went off in the carriage house. I took a walk out there and didn't see anything, but it's dark and I can't be a hundred percent sure no one was hiding in the bushes or someplace." His hands twisted in his lap. "All these alarms gave me the creeps."

"And then?" Kahn prodded.

"Then these two cops show up. They said there was some kind of disturbance in the courtyard and they needed to investigate. And, I thought, 'Shit, yeah, I could use some backup here.' So I let them in."

Once inside, the fake police continued to display convincing authority, maintaining control over the situation. They ordered the guard out from behind the desk where he could have access to the museum's only external alarm button. They handcuffed him and when the other guard on duty appeared, they handcuffed him, too. In short order the guards were in the basement, bound hand and foot, their heads wrapped in duct tape, handcuffed to pipes some distance apart. Hours later, a guard from the day shift found them.

"Have you been a museum guard long?" Kahn asked.

"A while."

"This your only job?"

"I told you. I'm at Berklee." Berklee College of Music.

"And that's it?"

"I'm in a band and we play gigs around town."

"On nights you're not working or…?"

"No, I can get to the museum after."

"Do you ever come to work drunk? Or after a few beers?"

The young man glanced at the other detectives, then out the door. "No way."

"Stoned?"

Now he squirmed in the chair. "Once or twice."

"Were you drunk or stoned last night?"

"No, man. I was at the performance lab until late. You can check."

The note a detective made suggested they would.

"Anyway," the guard continued, "the Irish bands had all the gigs last night." He tossed his head and his long hair rearranged itself behind his shoulders.

The second guard added little and when these interviews were over, Kahn turned to his detectives. "Well?"

"Not real Boston cops," one said. "Too organized."

"I'd say mafia. Some low-level mopes just starting out," another said.

Kahn reflected. "Shouldn't we consider other possibilities? Mafia's too easy."

"That's what the FBI will focus on," the first detective said. "That's their hammer."

"Their hammer?" the other one said in a what-the-hell tone.

"To a hammer, everything's a nail. Mafia. That's their hammer."

"And here they come," Kahn said, pointing toward the door where six men in suits strode in.

The museum's security system recording revealed the thieves entered at 1:24 a.m. and stayed inside for eighty-one minutes. They made two trips to their vehicle with the loot and on their way out, they snatched the videotape for the side-door camera. The physical evidence Kahn and his men observed indicated that rather than carry the largest paintings out in their frames, some of which were several feet on a side, they cut them away, leaving behind broken glass and shredded canvas.

"Look what a mess they made," a curator said.

"Pretty good job, though, for men probably wearing gloves," Kahn said.

"What I don't understand," she said, "is why they took what they did. Some of the works they stole—like the two Degas drawings—are not particularly valuable. Relatively speaking. And yet they left other works worth so much more, including the Titian, the *Europa*." She snorted, thinking of it. *The Rape of Europa* was art-world shorthand for the looting of artworks in Nazi-occupied countries and now the plunderers struck here in Isabella Gardner's beautiful sanctuary. Under her breath she said, "Rape. Exactly what it feels like."

She wasn't the last to point out the odd assortment of targets, which led the FBI and other authorities to conclude the thieves were amateurs who didn't know what they were doing.

Rome, Autumn, 1989

Some months before this record-shattering theft, Amit Madoor received a significant visitor at his Rome shop. The woman handed him a postcard-sized guide to the Isabella Stewart Gardner Museum that she'd brought from Boston. "You'd love it. The museum looks like a Renaissance Venetian palace," she said. "So elegant, yet informal. Like someone's home."

"Interesting." Madoor accepted the guide, intrigued by the implications of "informal."

"The painting on the front is Isabella Gardner herself in Venice. Isn't it lovely?"

"Indeed. She looks like a bird about to take flight." Madoor turned the small guide's pages, which described the museum's most important holdings and where the visitor would find them. He flipped back and forth to the floor plan inside the front cover.

"Keep it. I have no plans to return to the U.S.," his friend said.

"May I?" Madoor clutched the guide in both hands as if it were as precious as the objects it described. "It is really quite remarkable."

⚔ ⚔ ⚔ ⚔

Amit Madoor's antiquities shop on the Via in Selci—a narrow curving one-way Roman street between the Colosseum and the Basilica di Santa Maria Maggiore—attracted foot traffic from the western corner near the Cavour Metro station and the piazza at the eastern end, where five streets jumbled together. Yet it was not so near the main tourist attractions nor so elegant as to be in the high-rent district.

For some days after Madoor received the Gardner museum guide, tourists attracted to the shop window encountered a discreet "Closed" sign. Inside, Madoor was fully occupied with a series of lengthy long-distance telephone calls. Telephone security concerns being what they are in Italy, he took great care not to say directly what his business was. The people on the other end of the line whom his father recommended were quick and cooperative, even eager, once they understood his proposition and his guarantees.

They probably would not have understood the situation this way, but Madoor was turning the role of "fence" on its head, representing them—the buyers—in the world of gray-to-black art commerce, letting them create his shopping list. Madoor knew as well as anyone that stealing valuable artworks is child's play compared to disposing of them afterwards. By assuring the market was there before a theft, he dramatically reduced its downside risks. *If* he could find people brazen enough to carry it off.

Fez, Morocco, the 1970s

His father's stall could be found deep in the medina, squeezed between a seller of a thousand brilliant colors of thread and a dentist whose painted sign bore a smile with an improbable number of teeth. Standing outside the stall, 13-year-old Amit Madoor greeted customers from all over the world. The shop sold silver rings and bracelets, but what made the family's fortune were the other services his father provided. These were discussed in a back room and perhaps it was the smoke and fumes from the nearby ironworkers's stalls that brought tears to the customers's eyes.

Did a man need a passport in another name? An entry visa? More important, sometimes, an exit visa? Permission to travel? Did a woman seek the name of a border official who could be bribed? Men pushed wrinkled documents and envelopes stuffed with money across the table; women held out velvet pouches heavy with jewelry.

At least for a time, his father was the most important person in the world to these people. As he worked out what would be needed, Amit saw the light return to their eyes. Negotiations concluded, his older brother—Rashid's father—would take customers by the arm and escort them through the dark and crowded passageways. Their steps became surer, their backs straighter as his brother walked them to safety.

These customers were former confidants of the Shah of Iran, supported Nasser in Egypt or rapacious governments anywhere in the developing world. They stole public money and lucrative corporate secrets, escaping disaster by sheer luck or because governments changed hands or their replacements didn't want to risk exposure of their own dirty dealings. Over the years, the customers's politics and crimes changed, but not their desperation. In the world parade of bloody regimes and criminal conspiracies they found themselves on the wrong side of the street. Yet through attenuated family connections or relationships established in dusty trading posts or a friend of a friend of a friend, they ended up at a particular stall in the Fez medina.

One night, as they were closing the shop, Amit asked his father why he did what he did. "That man just here, that Javier Julima," Amit said, "he is very bad. Why do you help people like that?"

His father stopped his evening tasks to take his son's chin in his hand and said, "It is not up to me to judge a man's whole lifetime, the part that is to come. Think, Amit. If I sent him away without help, he would be killed within a week. He would die with all his sins on his heart and no chance to redeem himself. Our family gave him that chance and he may yet do some good in the world." As he spoke, Amit's father emptied the shop's cash register, putting the money in a zipper-bag he hid inside his *djellaba*.

"But will he?" Amit picked up the bag of oranges they were taking home to his mother and went to stand outside the shop while his father rolled down the overhead door and locked it.

"Some do. And, as long as they are alive, they have that opportunity. But if they do not, then I do not feel bad having taken their money. That does some good right here at home. Either way, there is a seed of good in what we do."

He put his arm around his son's shoulder and they walked home together. As they entered the house, his father put a coda on his reflections, saying, "No matter what path you follow in life, Amit, keep that seed alive. Even if you must do some bad thing, sweeten your act with good."

Copley Plaza, Boston
March 18, 1990, 6 p.m.

Madoor watched television as he ate another room-service dinner in his hotel. The story of the unthinkable robbery at the Isabella Stewart Gardner Museum led the evening news. He saw the museum's director plead for the return of the stolen artworks. When she said they might be damaged if not properly cared for, he stabbed his fork at her. As if he wouldn't protect his investment. His father's investment!

Boston's chief of police came on screen, confident of an early close to the case,but was metaphorically if not literally elbowed aside by the head of the local FBI office. They were searching strenuously for fingerprints. Madoor rolled his eyes. They were checking their organized crime database and investigating the whereabouts of known art thieves. Madoor sighed. Even looking internationally. He raised an eyebrow, then returned attention to his lamb chops.

The museum director reappeared to narrate a hastily assembled slide show of the stolen works. There they were again—the three Rembrandts (*too bad no one requested that other self-portrait*, he muttered, *what a lost opportunity!*), the Vermeer, the Manet, the Flinck (for many years thought to be another Rembrandt, the director said), the ancient Chinese bronze, the eagle from atop a Napoleonic banner (*the emperor's descendant will be disappointed we cannot provide the banner itself*) and five Degas drawings.

His fork clattered to his plate when among the Degas slides appeared not just the three drawings with horses, requested by a client trying to replicate an English country house in the Lebanese mountains, but also two studies called "Program for an Artistic Soiree." These drawings weren't on Madoor's list and they weren't in the cache Jack and Isaac delivered to him. He peered at the television.

Madoor finished the chops and started his salad as the nightly news drifted to more mundane matters: an impending City Council flap, another environmental roadblock in planning the Big Dig and the strangulation murder of an auto upholstery repair shop owner. In broken English, the man's distraught wife said a rush job kept her husband working through the night. That was all she knew.

Madoor was pleased she followed the script on the note he left her, accompanied by an envelope thick with cash. She added only, "He was an artist," with unintended irony. Madoor shook his head sadly.

In the background of this footage, filmed outside the workshop where the body was found, stretched a row of grimy ramshackle buildings, their rolling doors shut tight. These spaces predominantly housed dodgy auto parts businesses—thinly disguised chop-shops—and both for practical reasons and out of long habit, their mostly immigrant owners avoided the police. Even if they possessed information, they wouldn't share it and, anyway, there was no reason for them to mention the two pristine 1950s Cadillacs momentarily parked in their alley the evening before.

Madoor sensed indifference ran both ways and the death of the Algerian upholsterer would fade quickly from official attention. As the anchorwoman's capsule news summary reminded viewers, the Boston police had bigger fish to fry.

He switched off the television. They'd done it. He closed his eyes and let the enormity of the accomplishment fill him. Until he saw the museum director on television and the B-roll of the empty places on the Gardner's jacquarded walls, the theft didn't seemed quite real.

In memory the events of the night before appeared as a sequence of separate scenes that began when the surgical residents appeared out of the darkness and transferred the rolled-up paintings and other objects to the trunk of his rental car.

"We threw the plastic badges away," Jack said. "The toy guns, too. No place close to where we live. We'll red-bag the costumes in the morning."

"Red bag?" Madoor asked.

"They'll be on their way to the incinerator by noon. Nobody's going to root around in bags of medical waste," Isaac said.

In the next scene, Madoor stood in the shop smelling of leather and new vinyl admiring the Cadillacs. As the upholsterer sewed the artworks into the seat cushions, Madoor repeated his silent promise to take care of the man's family.

He relived the night's most difficult moment, the one that led to the body crumpled on the shop floor staring into eternal nothingness.

He saw the parking lot a few blocks away from the shop where he drove first one and then the other Cadillac and waited for Rashid to arrive. And finally, he recalled the activity on the dock as the Evergreen container was loaded, sealed and put aboard the ship.

Now he planned to stay here in his hotel until the *Annamarie* sailed. Once she was out of the harbor, he would fly to JFK and be on the next Rome-bound plane. He picked up his book and read one or two more pages, but the mystery of the Degas drawings kept creeping into his thoughts. They were quite similar and he could picture them on the walls of two success-ful surgeons on opposite coasts, reminders of their great escapade and their ongoing mutual need to keep quiet. In the unlikely event anyone asked about them, they could say, "Reproductions. Not bad, though." It was the response people would expect, surely.

But just as likely, he could imagine the drawings were a false clue, a police trap for the inevitable ransom-seekers. Taking these two minor pieces off display would be a small sacrifice for the Gardner, compared to what was truly lost.

✗ ✗ ✗ ✗

Monday morning a bored African American woman brought Madoor's room service breakfast and the newspaper. Like everyone else at the hotel, she never connected this quiet guest with the *Globe*'s lurid headlines.

Around noon, Jack called. "Just wanted you to know. Those accounts you set up for Isaac and me seem to be working. I just paid off one of my loans, the smallest one."

"Your money is all there. But remember, you will want spend only a little at a time for now."

"Got it. And we'll remember to keep complaining about our finances, too. Old habits are hard to break. I didn't realize…" Jack paused. "When I could finally pay that loan off, it meant a lot, really. It was like, I don't know, freedom, or…"

Madoor coughed and Jack said, "Isaac and I are taking your advice. We're looking forward, not back."

"That is best."

These two doctors both would have successful careers. They would never commit another such robbery. They would never be arrested for some crime and inveigled to trade freedom for information and they would never ever confess to a loose-lipped cellmate or prison stoolie. They would fly strato-spheres above suspicion for their entire lives.

"One bit of advice, though," Jack said. "A box-cutter is a piss-poor tool. Makes a crappy cut. Not what I'm used to."

"Hmmm." Madoor acknowledged. "Best of luck to you, Dr. Jack. To you and Isaac. In your careers you will help many, many people. I'm glad to have helped you get your start. Now, be content and do good."

"We will. Thank you."
And enjoy your Degas. If you have them.

Conley Terminal, Boston
Tuesday, March 20, noon

Madoor stood outside the terminal's chain-link fence. The *Annamarie's* smokestack loosed a puff of black smoke, the ship shuddered and it glided away from the dock to join the traffic in Boston Harbor. He raised his hand in salute to the ship, its hundreds of shipping containers, the two Cadillacs and the priceless haul from history's largest property theft.

Victoria Weisfeld is the author of seven published short stories, including two in the *Ellery Queen's Mystery Magazine* and one in the literary journal *Big Muddy*. She is a reviewer for the UK website, CrimeFictionLover.com and a member of Sisters in Crime, the Liberty States Fiction Writers Group and the Public Safety Writers Association. Her website, www.vweisfeld.com, includes timely articles of interest to readers, writers, movie- and theater-goers and observers of the chaotic 21st century.

IDYLLWILD

Michael Hemmingson

1.

Ex-cop Sean Talmadge—retired five years now—wouldn't let it go, and continued to harass me over a missing persons case he was convinced I was guilty of, going back seventeen years. When he was a homicide detective with the Hermosa Beach Police Department (northwest of Los Angeles), he followed me in his off hours and kept me under surveillance, albeit any evidence pointing toward the disappearance of my ex-lover, a friend of Talmadge's daughter. He retired three years ago but continued to haunt and harass me; he was no longer with the police department and claimed he was a licensed private detective and working for a client to find out what happened to Nicole Rense—that's the name of my ex-girlfriend. Talmadge's "client" was himself; the man was obsessed with me in a most unhealthy manner.

I moved from Hermosa Beach to the mountain community called Idyllwild in Riverside County. My father owned a pre-fab trailer in the retirement community Pine Grove and when he passed, I inherited the place. I am not retirement age but the park allows those under fifty-five to live there if a property is from inheritance. Six months after I moved to the quiet, cozy Idyllwild community, Sean Talmadge, age 65, moved into a trailer on the other side of the golf course from where I lived. I tried complaining to property management and they said he purchased the lot and pre-fab with a solid bank loan and he had every right to live here; more, in fact, because he was a senior citizen and I, age 44, was not.

I would have moved to another state, or across the country to the east coast, but I did not have the finances. I lived off disability benefits, the pittance the government allotted me, for injuries in the first Gulf War. With a prosthetic right leg and right arm, I was not exactly employable in the real world. Even if I could move far away, Talmadge would most likely follow me. He followed me when I flew to Las Vegas once; have no idea how he found out I was there and what hotel I was staying at—but there he was, in the casino in Circus Circus. "Oh, hey, Steven Vance," he said, acting surprised, "what a *coincidence* running into you." Right. "So," he said, patting me on the back, his breath smelling of vodka, "you here for some gambling or did you stash Nicki's body somewhere in Vegas? Lots of unsolved murders here in Vegas, eh?"

He was a heavy drinker. When he was still a cop, I filed several harassment complaints with the Hermosa Police Department. I had one interview with some lady from Internal Affairs; I suggested his drinking problem had made him delusional and obsessed. Talmadge did not stop bothering me; I knew his friends in the department simply looked the other way, and Talmadge most likely convinced them I was responsible for whatever happened to Nicole Rense.

2.

I met Nicole a year before I joined the Marines and was shipped to Kuwait in 1991. She was 20, second year of college, and I was 22. We had a rollercoaster relationship: one week madly in love, the other vehemently fighting. The passion made for some memorable times in the bedroom. She was angry and upset that I had joined the Corp. *"Why* do you want to be a stupid *jar*head?" she asked me with confusion. "You're gonna get *killed* over there," she said with concern. "Don't expect *me* to wait for *you,"* she said with spite.

I told Talmadge many times: "She broke up with me. She said she met some guy and was taking off to Vegas with him."

"So who is this 'guy'?" he would ask.

"I have no idea."

"Because he doesn't exist."

"She could have been lying."

"He's a fabrication of your imagination. What did you do to Nicki?"

"Nothing."

"Where is her body?"

"I have no idea."

"We're going to find out the truth eventually."

"When you do, let me know."

I was free of him when I went to the Middle East; there, I lost an arm and a leg from a landmine that the HumVee I was in drove over. Two men in my platoon died. For a long time I wished I had gone with them. I had to come home a crippled "hero." I did nothing heroic in Kuwait and Iraq. No one did.

3.

My handicapped status did not deter Talmadge from continuing his harassment, surveillance, and constant questioning and badgering. He was convinced I had something to do with Nicole's vanishing because his daughter, Lisa, told him so; she said Nicole was afraid of me, that I had physically hurt her.

"Something you must understand about Nicole," I said one time, when he brought me into the station and put me in an interview room, "she was into the rough stuff. She was into BDSM. She was *kinky."*

The look on his face was priceless: the shock, the disgust. "You're making that up," he said, making a fist; I knew he wanted to punch me in the mouth.

He refused to believe the truth about a young woman who had been friends with his daughter since they were both nine. I should have told him some dark nastiness I knew about Lisa, things Nicole had told me...

4.

I could feel his eyes whenever I took to the golf course. When I went to the community pool and relaxed in the Jacuzzi, he would show up and swim laps. He always kept his distance, never engaged conversation. I didn't know what he thought he'd find; perhaps he expected me to fall apart, drop to my knees and confess my crime because the weight of guilt was too heavy on my heart and I needed forgiveness.

When I drove into town for groceries and a liquor store run, or to have a burger and beer at the local grill, he would follow me in his beat up flatbed truck, do his shopping at the same time, or having a steak and vodka tonic at the local grill.

One day I decided *enough,* it was time to confront him.

5.

I drove east, on the highway, and headed down the mountain for the desert. I looked in the rearview: he kept his distance, but his truck was there, pacing. I pressed on the pedal and lost him for a while; I slowed down and let him catch up. I speeded; slowed down, let him come back. I toyed with him for three hours, wondering if he had enough gas for this, if he kept a full tank like I did.

I drove through Palm Springs, then to Indio, and headed southeast toward the Salton Sea. It was four in the afternoon and the sun was blazing hot. The car thermometer read 113. I had AC. Did Talmadge? Was he sweating it up in that old truck?

We were the only vehicles for miles in both directions, in the middle of the desert, the rancid smell of the Salton Sea muggy and thick. I was looking for a certain mile marker. When I passed it, I drove two hundred feet and stopped. This was the place I wanted.

This was the exact place I had planned.

I got out of my car and he got out of his truck. His skin was bright pink and his body covered in sweat. He approached me quickly, stomping his feet on the scorching hot pavement. He had a revolver in his hand, a .38 Smith and Wesson. He pointed the weapon at my chest, hand shaking. I worried he would accidentally pull the trigger.

"Did you hide her body somewhere around here?" he demanded. "Is that why you stopped?"

"I stopped because you've been following me, Talmadge. Why won't you let this go?"

"I loved her," he said like a croak, and then he began to cry. The heat and stress was too much for him. "God help me, I loved that sweet beautiful girl."

So that was it. I remember Nicole telling me about an older man who was obsessed with her, in love with her. She never said who it was. "It's really kinda sad," she'd said.

"Something you should know," I said slowly, "I had a threesome with Nicole and Lisa. That's right: I *made love* to *your* daughter. Once. Just once, with Nicki there."

That was a lie but I knew it would strike him deep. I should have told him this before. His face paled. "You…" He couldn't speak. His eyes bulged. "No," he moaned. He dropped the gun and fell to his knees, grabbing at his chest, trying to breathe.

I moved toward him. "Something the matter, old man?"

"My…in my…cab," he wheezed. "Pills. My…nitro…please…"

I walked to his truck. I took my time, hobbling on my prosthetic leg. I opened the cab door and spotted a pillbox on the passenger seat. I opened it. There were eight sections for vitamins and medicine: iron and calcium, Vicodin and nitro.

Talmadge was lying on the ground. I stood over him, holding the pillbox over his head. He reached up and pleaded, "Pill…please…"

"First I want to tell you something," I said. "I'm going to give you the confession you've been waiting seventeen years for. Yeah, I buried Nicole near here. Sweet little beautiful Nicki." I gestured. "About half a mile out there, middle of the desert. You've been right all along, Sean. You can die knowing that, and knowing you won't be able to do a thing about it."

He began to violently shake. He wanted to get up. He wanted his gun. His heart would not cooperate with his desire for justice.

I picked up the .38.

"I should show you mercy. Instead, I am going to stand here and watch you slowly die. For the seventeen years of hell you gave me. I lost two limbs for this country and what do I come back to? *You.* Was Nicole there for me? She said she loved me, she said we were soul mates, until I joined the Marines. She broke up with me; said she met some guy at a party and was going to Vegas with him for the weekend. I'm sure it was a lie to hurt me, to show me she was serious about letting me go. She came to my apartment to tell me that. I was hammering some nails into the wall to put up a painting and I used that hammer, slammed it into her head. I crushed her skull. I put her body in the trunk of my car; it was easy, she was petite and skinny, as you know. I drove out here, I knew the desert, I knew I could bury her out here and no one would ever find her. And that's what I did. Her bones are out there, buried. I could go out there and dig her up, you know. I left a large rock on her grave, in case I ever needed to move her body."

By the time I was done talking, he was dead.

I leaned down. "Goodbye, Detective Talmadge."

I left him there. I got into my car, taking his gun, and drove back to Idyllwild.

6.

A trucker came across his body and called the highway patrol. I saw a news item on TV and word around the retirement community was that Mr. Talmadge had died of a heart attack out by the Salton Sea. There was an obituary in the local weekly.

I thought I was free now; I could live my uneventful life in peace. The first visit I received was three weeks later, by his daughter Lisa. I had met her a few times when I dated Nicole. The years had not been kind to her; the sprite teenage girl in my memory was now a tired, plump real estate agent and mother of three, two husbands behind her.

"Hello, Steven," she said.

I acted like I didn't know her.

"It's me, Lisa Talmadge. Well, Harrison. That was my second married name. I was Talmadge."

"Oh yes. *Lisa.* How are you doing?" I pretended "how strange this is."

She gestured behind her. "I'm collecting my father's belongings. He passed away...did you know that?"

She was playing me. I replied, "Yes, I heard. My condolences."

She stood there, waiting for me to invite her in, the civil thing to do. So I did. She walked past me and looked around, taking inventory of my Spartan existence. She saw the extra prosthetic limbs leaning against a bookcase. "So you were injured in the war," she said.

"Yeah. Some war."

"It must have been painful." Her voice was cold.

"Can I get you something? Soda, water, soda water? A beer?"

She turned and glared. "Let's cut the bogus nicey-nice, Steven."

"Let's."

"I know why my father moved out here."

"To stalk me."

"Not *stalk.* Investigate."

"Your dad was a sick man. Senile, delusional. You must know this."

"What I know," she said, "is that you did something to Nicki. My best friend. I knew about your violence."

"And hers? You must have known she was..."

"I *knew* what she liked." She was uncomfortable saying that, her face going red. "I know she went to see you, to dump you in person. She thought you deserved that much, no Dear John letter or a phone call."

"She never came to my apartment to tell me anything," I said calmly. "She broke up with me on the phone. I told your dad this—hundreds of times."

"I talked to her the night before. I didn't hear from her again. No one did, not her folks, other friends. *No one.*"

"She took off with some guy."

"Yeah, she said she met a new guy but she didn't go anywhere with him."

I felt a tinge of pain—so the other guy *was* true.

"My dad talked to that guy and the guy said she never showed up for the Vegas trip."

That bitch…that cheating bitch…

"What happened to my dad?" she asked sharply.

"He had a heart attack."

"My dad checked in every day on what he was doing. 'Just in case' he always said. He was determined to find out the truth and put you away."

"Like I said, he was a disturbed man with an obsession."

Should I tell her what her father confessed, that he "loved" Nicole in a way a man should not love his daughter's friend? I could say maybe he killed Nicole and was trying to pin the old crime on an innocent man…

"He called from his cell phone and said he was following your car," Lisa said. "The same day he was found in the middle of nowhere, rotting in the hot sun."

"Lisa, I'm sorry, but that is not true. I have not been out of this trailer in three months, other than to go into town for groceries."

If anyone in this park saw me drive out of town, saw Talmadge follow me in his truck, noticed that I came home late, my alibi would shatter. This was a community of tired old people, however, who were lost in the past or preoccupied with their favorite TV shows.

"He was on to you and you knew it."

"I'm going to have to ask you to leave," I told her.

I held the door open. She walked out. The tension off her body was like a wave of knives.

"Your day will come, Steven," she said.

I sighed and feigned weariness. "Again, my condolences about your father. He may have been mentally ill, but deep down he was a good man."

"The hell with you," she said, walking away fast, back to her father's trailer, back to picking up what was left of his life.

7.

I had committed no crime, unless withholding medication from a heart attack victim was a crime. No one could prove that; there were no witnesses on that empty stretch of road. I did steal his registered handgun, and that could be construed a criminal act. That night, after Lisa's visit, I dismantled the handgun and drove back to the desert, burying the pieces every five miles.

I kept one bullet as a trophy, like I had kept Nicole's hair clip.

Hindsight: perhaps I should have broke into Talmadge's trailer; he most likely had a file on me, surveillance photos, notes on his theories. Then again, if I had removed anything like that and his daughter knew about it, suspicion would fall on me.

I was surprised that Nicole's remains had not been found by now. I had waited for it all these years, for the warrant and handcuffs, if her bones could even be identified. The crushed skull would indicate murder. Maybe one day she would be found, and I would be long gone from this earth.

I simply wanted to live the rest of my days in peace.

8.

Five months went by. I expected another visit from Lisa. Her father's trailer went up for sale and was purchased by a couple from Canada. They were nice people and I chatted with them by the pool a few times. They had always dreamed of retiring to nether regions of California.

Five months, and then I was paid a visit by a Los Angeles County Sheriff's detective named Harold Kent. He gave me his card, showed me his badge and ID. He asked if he could come in and talk to me. I said certainly. "How can I help you, Detective Kent?"

"May I sit down? It's pretty damn hot out."

"I have AC," I said. I reached for the control on the wall and turned on the cold air. "Can I get you anything? Water, soda, soda water? Beer?"

"If you have some cold water," he said, sitting at the card table in the living room area. An antique manual typewriter was on the card table; one day I would write a memoir about the Gulf War and Nicole.

I got us both small bottles of water from the fridge. I sat across from him.

"Thank you," he said, gulping the water down. He was a heavy-set man in his mid-50s, probably more used to deskwork than the field. I looked at his card: he was in the economic crimes division. Deskwork, tracking down embezzlers and bad checks.

"You were a Jarine in Gulf One," he said. "I was there, manning radar at CentCom in Saudi Arabia."

"Army?"

"Reserves."

"Would you like another water?"

"Eh? I'm fine, thanks. Let me get to it, Mr…"

"Call me Steve."

"It's about Sean Talmadge. You know who he is—was."

"Yes, he lived across the golf course."

"Sean and I were good friends; we were partners in a patrol car twenty-five years ago. He trained me, had seven years seniority. He made detective before me, the smart bastard. He wanted homicide; I wanted white-collar kicks. I knew he was keeping an eye on you, convinced you had something to do with a girl's disappearance. His daughter calls me, she says you had something to do with her father's death."

"He had a heart attack is what I heard."

"Yes, a massive coronary. It was bound to happen, he didn't take care of himself."

"She came to see me and made accusations," I said. "I did not cause her father's heart attack."

"She's upset. She also thinks you are responsible for her missing friend."

"Is that why you're here? Are you investigating me now?"

He held out his hands. "Not my jurisdiction. And I'm not homicide. I'm just here to get Lisa off my back. You must understand, she won't stop bugging me unless I came out here and had a talk with you."

"I understand," I said.

"I'm sure she'll come to her senses, that her dad died naturally and these things happen."

"I feel for her loss."

"Hopefully she'll be satisfied when I tell her my opinion is: you're a wounded vet living quietly out here."

"That's me."

He stood up. "Thank you for your understanding."

"Anytime."

We shook hands.

I didn't believe him. Never trust a cop.

I watched him from the window. He was taking a good look at my plot, my car. He looked back at my trailer.

9.

I was on my guard. After six weeks, I again thought this mess was done with. Never underestimate the determined. Lisa Harrison neé Talmadge broke into my trailer, a gun in her hand. She wasn't stealth about it; I heard the sound of glass breaking, my side door opening. I grabbed the baseball bat I kept by the bed and rushed to the living room. Lisa turned on the light and smiled at the sight of me, holding the bat, she holding the gun: a .9mm Glock. She probably found it with her father's belongings when she came by to pick up his stuff.

"I know how to use a gun," she said, "Daddy taught me."

"What's the meaning of this?" I asked, wondering if I should rush her, if she had it in her to shoot.

"Drop the bat, you murderer."

I saw in her eyes intent. Yeah, she would shoot me; it had taken her months to get up the nerve to come here.

I put the bat down. "Take it easy, we can talk about this…"

"Oh yes, *we will talk.*"

"I know you are upset about your father…"

"I have been *upset* nearly two decades about my friend. *My best friend.* That you took away from me. What did you *do* with her?"

"Lisa, look," I said, stepping forward.

"One more step and you're dead."

"All right then, you want me to say it? I killed her. I killed Nicole. I didn't plan to; it just happened; I lost my control. She broke up with me and I had a hammer and I used it." How strange it felt, a relief: to say it out loud, to tell someone my darkest secret, like I had told her father out by the Salton Sea.

She wasn't expecting my confession. "Just like Daddy said."

"That's right, Lisa. Sean Talmadge was correct all along. But did you know your father was in love with Nicole? Your best friend? That he wanted—"

"Shut up with your lies!"

She stumbled. Was she drunk? Her father was a drinker; I remember Nicole mentioning that Lisa liked her wine a little too much.

"What did you do with her body?"

"She's out in the desert." I had an idea. I said, "I can take you to her."

"What?"

"I can take you to her grave, and you can vindicate your dad. You'll be the hero. I want to turn myself in and confess," I lied to her. "I want to pay for what I did. Your dad will be a hero, so will you. It is time for me to do this."

"Okay," she said. "Is it far?"

"Not far," I lied again.

"I'll shoot you, I really will, if you try any monkey business."

"We'll just need a flashlight and a shovel, okay? Don't get nervous."

She followed me as I got a flashlight from the kitchen and a shovel from the back of the trailer. I could smell booze on her breath.

"We can take my car," I said.

"Wait, I don't know," she said, "let's wait until morning when the sun—"

She stumbled on one of her feet. Drunk. I swung the shovel around, hitting her on the side of the head. She dropped the gun and looked at me with surprised terror. I swung the shovel again.

10.

I took Lisa out to the desert to be with her friend. I could not find the exact spot in the dark. It was close enough. The sun was just coming up when I finished digging a hole. I dumped Lisa into the hole and covered her up.

I stopped for breakfast driving back to Idyllwild. I would have to pack some things, go somewhere else, another state. Or I could just stay put and play dumb. I would need to wipe the trailer down for prints, fix the broken glass on the side door; look for her car in the retirement park, or outside it, wherever she left it. I didn't know what she drove; I would need to keep an eye on a parked car in the same spot over the next week. *This could be done, this will work...*

11.

"Don't join the Marines," Nicole had said. "Stay here with me, or go and never have me. Your choice."

12.

Choices, I thought when I arrived home, to find several Riverside Sheriff vehicles and one unmarked car parked around my trailer.

Harold Kent was there, sporting a glib smile. The sheriff deputy handed me a warrant, giving them carte blanche to search my trailer, which they had already done when I was gone.

Kent held in his hand what they were seeking: a cell phone. Another deputy had two items bagged: Nicole's hair clip, Talmadge's bullet: my momentos.

Lisa had left her phone on when we had our exchange, placed on the card table by the typewriter and I had not noticed; everything I said was on Kent's voice mail at the LAPD.

My lawyer is working on getting the recording tossed out: it was obtained by a citizen, there was no warrant for such, and a recording in possession of the LAPD was out of jurisdiction—they did not know where Nicole was murdered, she vanished from Hermosa Beach, and they had no body—for a cold case crime and the case of the now missing Lisa Harrison. Search parties were sent into the desert, but the desert was too vast, no graves, body or bones turned up.

Nevertheless, I have decided to confess. It is time. I will give my allocution to the court: my crime seventeen years ago, what really happened with Sean Talmadge, where I buried both Nicole and Lisa...

13.

Or maybe not.

The judge has excluded the voice mail as unlawfully obtained evidence. Without it, my lawyer says, they cannot hold me. The lawyer is filing a motion to have charges dropped. I will be back home soon, in Idyllwild.

✗

Michael Hemmingson (July 12, 1966 – January 9, 2014) was a novelist, short story writer, literary critic, cultural anthropologist, qualitative researcher, playwright, music critic and screenwriter. He died in Tijuana, Mexico on 9 January 2014. The reported cause was cardiac arrest. This was one of his last stories.

MOTIVE

Marc Bilgrey

The call came in at midnight. I was asleep, dreaming of my ex-wife. In the dream she still loved me, and hadn't run away with Morton Young, the town pharmacist. The phone kept ringing. I turned on the light on my night table, glanced at the alarm clock, and reached for the receiver.

"Sheriff Alden," I said.

"It's Deputy Douglas."

"It's after midnight, Deputy, what's going on?"

"I'm sorry to disturb you, Sheriff, but there's been a murder."

"A murder?" I'd been Sheriff of Forest Grove for ten years. The last murder had taken place nine years earlier. Domestic violence case. A wife killed her husband in self-defense. He'd been beating her. The jury took half an hour to acquit her.

"Sheriff?"

"Yes. Who got killed and where?"

"The victim is Zak Olin. I'm at his farm. He was found by his daughter, Maggie."

"Secure the crime scene. No one goes in or out. I'll be right there."

I put on my uniform, went outside, and got into my squad car. Who would want to kill Zak Olin? I wondered, as I pulled the car out of my driveway. I'd known Zak Olin my whole life. He was a year ahead of me in high school. He was a nice guy; quiet, kept to himself. He lived for his seventeen old daughter, Maggie. When Zak's wife died, seven years ago, after a long battle with cancer, the whole town showed up for her funeral. He never remarried. Everyone liked Zak. He grew corn and tomatoes, attended church regularly, loved his daughter. Zak and I were never very close, but when I'd see him at town meetings, or the supermarket, he'd always smile and say hello.

It occurred to me to turn on the siren and run the lights, but I figured, why wake folks up? Zak was dead. He wasn't going anywhere.

Ten minutes later, I pulled into the Olin farm. Deputy Earl Douglas was standing by his patrol car, which was parked in front of the house. Maggie Olin was on the porch, sitting on a wicker chair, crying. I went up to Earl and said, "How is she?"

"Pretty broken up. She called me a few minutes before I called you. I happened to be nearby. I was driving home from Riley's Bar." I gave him a look. "All I had was coffee."

"What happened?" I said, pointing to the house.

"She says she came home and found her father lying on the floor, all bloody, and dead. I took a quick look. Zak Olin's been hit over the head. Blunt force trauma."

"Poor bastard."

I went over to Maggie. She was still sobbing as I sat down on the chair next to her. She was a pretty girl; thin, black hair, brown eyes. She looked up at me and said:

"Who would want to do this?"

"That's what we're going to find out," I replied. "Your father was a good man." She wiped tears from her eyes with a tissue. "I need to ask you some questions, Maggie." She nodded. "I know you already talked to Deputy Douglas, but I have to hear it from you, okay?" She nodded again. "Tell me what happened."

She dabbed her eyes and said, "I was away for a few days on a sleepover in Hillridge, with my friend Francine Michaels. It's spring break. And I just got home, and I walk in and see my Dad on the floor..." She started crying again.

"You didn't touch anything, did you?" I asked.

"No, I went outside and called 911 on my cell."

"Did your father have any enemies?"

"Not that I know of. Everyone liked Dad."

"Okay," I said, standing, "now I want you to stay with Deputy Douglas for a few minutes while I go into the house."

She nodded. The front door was slightly ajar. There were no signs of forced entry. I pushed the door open and stepped into the living room. Zak Olin was lying on the floor. His skull had been bashed in. There was blood spatter near him, and bits of bone, and brain. It wasn't a pretty sight. I walked around the room. There didn't seem to be anything out of place. There were a few chairs, a couch, a coffee table, a couple of end tables, and lamps. Maybe whoever killed him rearranged things and tidied up afterwards.

I looked in the kitchen. On the counter, near the sink, was a cast iron frying pan. It looked clean, as if it had been washed recently. I went back into the living room, then upstairs to the master bedroom. I saw no signs of disturbance. I looked into Maggie's room, and that seemed untouched, too. I went back downstairs and over to the tan couch. I saw a small red smudge on the right armrest. It didn't look like lipstick, but I suppose it could have been. I got on my knees and crawled around on the floor. Near the leg of the left side of the couch, I found some dark grains of something. I smelled them. It was tobacco.

I went back outside the house, and over to Maggie. She was still sitting on the wicker chair, crying. Deputy Douglas was sitting next to her, trying to console her. When he saw me approach, he got up. I sat down and said: "How long were you away at your friend's place?"

"A week," she replied.

"Did your Dad smoke?"

"No."

"How about you?"

"No."

"Did your Dad or you know anyone who smokes?"

"I can't think of anyone."

"Is there someone in town you can stay with for a few days?"

"Why can't I stay here?"

"It's a crime scene now. We need to preserve it. It may take a few days to process."

"I can stay with my friend, Rachael Miller. She lives on Frog Pond Road."

"Call her, then Deputy Douglas will escort you there."

A few minutes later Maggie got into her car, and Deputy Douglas got into his squad car, and they drove off. I stood on the porch and watched till they both disappeared down the road. Then I took out my cell and called John Myers, the police chief in Brynton, the biggest city in the area. I apologized for the time I was calling, told him about the murder, and asked if he could spare his CS Unit to come down and process the crime scene. He told me that I was in luck, being how things had been quiet for a few days, where he was, and that he would send them immediately. I thanked him, gave him the address and directions, and hung up. I was taking no chances. I'd seen too many small town homicide investigations compromised because some local cop didn't have the resources or the know how to solve a case, and was too grandiose to admit he needed help. There's no substitute for the expertise of an experienced team, and that included a crime lab.

I went into my squad car and waited. Two hours later, I was woken up the sound of cars approaching. It was Meyer's Crime Scene Unit. I got out, introduced myself to the three men and two women, and took them into the house. I watched as they went to work, taking photos and videos, dusting for prints, and examining the blood spatter. They used portable luminal lights, tweezers, and tagged and bagged as they went. A few hours later, when they were done, the ME's office took the body away. After that, I placed a police seal on the front door, got into my car, and started driving home. I was exhausted and looking forward to getting some sleep. My cell rang. I put it on speaker.

"Sheriff Alden," I said.

"Sheriff, it's Ralph, stop by my office."

"Okay."

So much for sleep. I thought, now I had the mayor asking to see me. I drove into town and pulled up to his real estate office on Main Street. Ralph Todd's secretary, Betty, led me through his real estate office, and into the back room, where his private office was. Like many small towns, being mayor doesn't mean you quit your day job.

Ralph was just finishing a phone call, as I sat down in the client chair in front of his desk. As soon as he hung up he turned to me. "I heard about Zak Olin's murder. How's the investigation going?"

"I'll know more when I hear from Meyer's CSU team, the ME's office, and the lab guys."

"I heard that Olin just bought a few acres adjoining his property."

"You sold it to him?"

"My competitor across the street, Linda Rice."

I stood up. "Thanks, Ralph."

"One more thing, Dan, I'd really like you to solve this case."

"I would, too."

"Next year is an election year."

✗ ✗ ✗ ✗

I walked into Linda Rice's office and sat down across from her desk. She never took her eyes off her computer.

"Bad news about Zak Olin," she said. "You in the market for a bigger house, Sheriff? I have a nice Cape Cod in town that's a steal."

"I don't buy stolen property."

This got a quick glance from Rice, then she went back to her computer.

"I understand that you recently sold Zak Olin a piece of land."

"Fifteen acres adjoining his farm. He bought it last month. Elderly widow next door, Elsa Williams, owned it. The place had been in her family for decades."

"What made her sell?"

"Her son moved her into an assisted living facility in Oakville .Then he put the land on the market. I can't say I blame him, he works in the insurance business, lives in the next state; doesn't have much use for the old place. Olin was thrilled to buy it. He said, now he'd be able to have more room to grow different types of vegetables. I suppose somebody has to do it. Me? I just buy them in the produce section of the supermarket."

I stood up.

"I have a nice Greek Revival just out of town," said Linda, "it's a good price. Hey, maybe you'll get married again."

"I don't think so."

"Is that a 'no' on the house, or on marriage?"

"Both," I said, as I walked out of her office.

The next office I stopped by was my own. I found my Deputy at his desk, talking on the phone, while he looked through some papers. When he saw me he ended the call.

"Sheriff," he said, "I got newspapers and TV news wanting a statement."

"Tell 'em that we don't comment on ongoing investigations."

"That's what I said."

"Good. If you want me, I'll be in Hillridge, checking out Maggie Olin's alibi."

"You don't think she had anything to do with her father's death, do you?"

"Of course not, but I have to follow up, anyway."

✗ ✗ ✗ ✗

I located Maggie Olin's friend, Fran Michaels, at her high school, in Hillridge. I talked to the principal, who had her come to his office. When she arrived, he left me alone with her. Fran was Maggie's age, blonde, blued eyed. She wore a white blouse and a pair of tight fitting jeans.

"Am I in some kind of trouble?" she asked, sitting down on a chair near the principal's desk.

"Not at all, I just need to ask you some questions about your friend, Maggie Olin."

"Is she okay?"

"She's fine, but her father's dead. He's been murdered."

"That's horrible. Who did it?"

"We're investigating that. Maggie stayed with you last week?"

"It was spring break. She went home last night."

"What'd you do all week?"

"We hung out with friends, went to the diner, went bowling, played miniature golf, went to the movies, stuff like that."

"Where was Maggie yesterday?"

"We went to a movie, then afterwards she went home."

"Anyone see you?"

She looked at me and squinted. "Sure, a lot of people saw us, why?"

"Were you with Maggie every hour of every day last week?"

"Well...."

"Did she ever go off on her own?"

"Uh, no."

"You sure about that?"

She looked away. "Does it really matter?"

"It might."

"Ummm...."

"If you withhold information during a homicide investigation you could be charged with obstruction. That might mean that you'd go to jail."

She swallowed. "Look, I promised I wouldn't tell anyone."

"Is it worth getting a criminal record for?"

"Okay, look, there was this boy..."

"A boy?"

"Yeah. Maggie was seeing him, but she didn't want her Dad to know."

"Why not?"

"He didn't like him."

"What's this boy's name?

"Tommy Wallace. Maggie made me swear—"

"Her Dad's dead now."

"Oh, yeah. Anyway, she would sneak off to see Tommy."

"How about yesterday, did they sneak off?"

"Yeah, we didn't really go to a movie. In fact, she was with him the whole weekend."

"Why didn't Maggie's Dad like this boy?"

"He drives a sports car; he's a smart ass, wrong side of the tracks, all the usual stuff. Oh, also, he's nineteen."

"Other than that, he's perfect. Give me his address."

"You won't tell Maggie or Tommy that I snitched on them, will you?"

"I'll try to keep you out of it, but I can't make any promises."

"You don't think that Tommy…."

"I don't think anything till I get more facts," I said, and got up to leave.

✗ ✗ ✗ ✗

I walked into Barrett's restaurant on Main Street, in downtown Hillridge, and asked the hostess, a woman in her sixties, with a name tag on her blouse that read, 'Bunny', where I could find Tommy Wallace.

"Tommy's on a break. Check the alley around back."

"A busboy on a break?"

"Slow day."

I went through the kitchen, opened a back door and stepped into an alley. A skinny young man was sitting by a trashcan smoking a joint. He took one look at me, got up and started running. I chased after him, grabbed him, pushed him against a brick wall, and cuffed him.

"W-what'd I do?" he asked.

"Let's start with resisting arrest, and move to possession of a controlled substance."

"It's a victimless crime."

"We'll see about that."

I put him in the back of my squad car and drove to the station. When we got there, I stuck him in the interrogation room, and let him sit alone while I went to my desk and punched his name into my computer. A few minutes later I went back into the interrogation room and sat down at the table. He looked at me then said:

"I don't get it. You drive all the way out to Hillridge to bring me in for one little cigarette?"

"Why don't we talk about Maggie Olin."

"Maggie? What about her?"

"You spent time with her last week. What I want to know is how much time?"

"I don't understand. "

"How long were you with Maggie this weekend?"

"Did her old man put you up to this?"

"Maybe if you're straight with me I might develop amnesia on the drug bust."

"Yeah, okay, I saw her every day last week. Saturday and Sunday we were at my uncle's cabin by the lake."

"Anyone see you there?"

"No."

"Wrong answer."

"Why are you—"

"Maggie's father, Zak Olin didn't like you."

"I knew that guy was behind this."

"If he was out of the way you wouldn't have to sneak around any more."

"What're you talking about?"

"He's dead."

"D-dead? How?"

"You killed him."

"I didn't kill anyone."

"You just steal cars and shoplift?"

"I was fourteen."

"Five long years ago."

We went in circles for a while but he never broke. All he did was profess his innocence, and his love for Maggie Olin. I couldn't decide if he was a good liar, or just plain innocent. I finally got up and left the room. I was watching Tommy sitting alone through the two-way mirror, when I was interrupted by Deputy Douglas.

"We got the preliminary report back from CSU," he said, handing it to me.

"That's good," I replied.

"What should we do with the suspect?"

"Stick him in the holding cell."

"What's the charge?"

"We don't have to charge him for twenty-four hours. But if anyone asks, resisting arrest will do for now."

I sat down at my desk and read through what CSU sent me. Zak Olin's tox screen was negative. Cause of death was cranial bleeding from blunt force trauma, consistent with a heavy, flat object, such as the cast iron frying pan in the Olin's kitchen. Latent found no prints, other than those of the deceased and his daughter. The lack of prints suggested that someone may have wiped the surfaces to obliterate evidence. There was no hair, fibers, or fluids found at the scene, other than those belonging to the vic. The tobacco turned out to be a Jamaican blend, called Allure. The red stain was analyzed, and proved to be a common food dye. There was also a fresh set of tire tracks in front of the house not belonging to either Zak Olin's car or his daughter's vehicle. These were plastered and a couple of photos were included. ME's preliminary report, based on lividity, put time of death between ten to twelve midnight on Saturday night, which meant by the time Maggie called us, her father had been dead for approximately twenty-four hours.

I walked out of my office, went through the squad room, and exited the station. There didn't seem to be an immense amount of evidence to go on. I walked up Main Street, then crossed over to the other side, and went into Chuck's News Store. Chuck Kanner was standing by the racks, putting out some new magazines. He saw me and smiled.

"Hi Sheriff, coming in to buy a lottery ticket? The prize is up to three million."

"Not today, Chuck."

"Too bad about Zak Olin, huh?"

"Yeah. Did he come in here, often?"

"Try never. Kept to himself."

"How about Maggie?"

"Ditto."

"Say, Chuck, I wanted to ask you, how's your pipe tobacco sales been, lately?"

"Slim to non-existent. Not a lot of pipe smokers in the area. Cigarettes, cigars, chewing tobacco. But pipes, not so much."

"You carry a brand of tobacco called Allure?"

"No, I don't carry it, but I can special order it for you."

"Nah, that's okay," I said, as I turned and started walking to the door.

"It's no bother," he said, "I already have one customer I order it for anyway."

I turned around and looked at Chuck.

"Ben Dunn," he said, "he teaches over at the community college."

✗ ✗ ✗ ✗

Forest Grove Community College didn't have a very big campus. I walked along the closely cropped grass, amid the faux Medieval buildings, and asked a couple of young women who were carrying books for directions. Five minutes later I stood in a hallway looking through the window of a door, and saw a man in his late fifties, at a desk, reading some papers. He had a greying beard and was dressed in a rumpled jacket, with patches on the elbows. Whether the jacket had been purchased that way, or they came later was anyone's guess. I knocked and walked inside.

"Mr. Dunn?" I asked.

"Yes?" he replied, looking up from his papers.

"I'm Sheriff Alden. Can I have a few minutes of your time?"

"Sure," he said, gesturing to a chair. "I know that some of my students take their papers off the internet, but I didn't realize it was a police matter."

I smiled. "You teach biology?"

"Not judging by my students's grades, but I try."

I looked at a small statue of a tyrannosaurus on his desk, then back at Dunn. "I'm doing some follow-up on a case."

"What has that got to do with me?"

"Where were you on Saturday night?"

"At home, correcting papers."

"Can anyone vouch for that?"

"I live alone."

"What kind of car do you drive?"

"A blue Chrysler, why?"

"Plate number?"

"HGE 2710, but I don't understand what…."

I looked at a framed picture above his desk. It was an old print, a portrait of a man. Dunn noticed my interest.

"It's Charles Darwin."

"Nice print."

"Thanks," he said, then, took a pipe out of a drawer, knocked it on the arm of his chair, and lit a match. "I hope you don't mind if I smoke, Sheriff."

"This building has a strict no smoking policy," I said. "You always break the law in front of the police?"

He looked at me, and blew out the match. "Okay, you talked me out of it."

"My father liked a good pipe after dinner, what kind of tobacco do you use?"

"It's a blend called Allure."

"How well did you know Zak Olin?"

"Who?"

"Owns a farm ten minutes from here."

"Why do you ask?"

"Just a routine investigation."

"I have to get back to marking papers."

"You do a lot of that."

"They won't mark themselves."

On my way out of the building, I saw a door with a sign on it that read, 'Lounge'. I went inside, and saw a woman standing by a counter, pouring herself a cup of coffee. She noticed me and said: "May I help you?"

"I'm Sheriff Alden."

"I'm Alice Vernon."

"Are you in the science department?"

"English."

"Do you know Ben Dunn?"

"Yeah."

"What's he like?"

"He doesn't talk much to me. All he's interested in is science. He has a one track mind."

"Who does he talk to?"

"No one that I know of."

In the parking lot I found Benn Dunn's car, went over to it, and took out the CSU photos of the tire prints that were found in front of Zak Olin's house. I knelt down at the rear driver's side tire and looked at it. The tread on the tire looked almost new; couldn't have been on the car too long.

✗ ✗ ✗ ✗

When I got back to my car, I called Judge Falco and asked him if he could get give me an order to dump Ben Dunn's financials, and phone records. When he asked me for probable cause, I told him about the tobacco, and the unverifiable alibi at the time of the murder. He said it was a stretch, but would grant it. I suppose it helps to play chess with the judge on his off hours, and not to win every game. After I hung up with him, I called Deputy Douglas and told him to get to work on Dunn's financials and LUDs (police jargon for local usage details of telephone activity).

I drove to Ben Dunn's neighborhood. He lived in a housing development near town. I parked on the corner up the block from Dunn's house, got out and started walking. I knocked on doors and asked everyone who answered if they had seen Dunn on Saturday night. No one had. I also asked if they knew of any friends that Dunn had. All his neighbors said the same thing: that Dunn was a loner. I was about to get back into my car, when I saw an old man walking a poodle.

"What's going on, Sheriff?" he asked.

"You know Ben Dunn?"

"I ought to, I live right across the street from him. Name's Ron Kohl."

"You happen to see him on Saturday night?"

"I was looking out my window at eight o'clock and noticed him drive off."

"When did he get back?"

"I wouldn't know. I go to bed at midnight, he was still out."

I drove on to the main road, and was on my way back to the station, when I got a call from Deputy Douglas. He'd gotten Dunn's financials and LUDs.

"This guy does pretty well for a prof," said Douglas.

"How's that?"

"Aside from his salary he gets lots of checks from an outfit called, Speak Easy."

"A bar?"

"No. I looked them up, it's a lecture bureau."

"What's he talk about, biology?"

"Well, he is a biology teacher."

"How about his phone?"

"Lots of local calls to one number. Reverend Tyler."

"Interesting, thanks."

I kept driving, and in a few minutes was back in town. I drove down Main Street, past the station and continued till I saw a big white church. I stopped in front of it, got out and went up the steps. Inside, Reverend Tyler's secretary Mary led me into his upstairs office, then left us alone. Rev. Tyler was sitting at his desk, tapping away at a computer. He stopped as I sat down, and smiled.

"Hi Sheriff. Just working on a sermon."

"Hope I'm not disturbing."

"No, I was due for a break, anyway. All the fire and brimstone was making me thirsty." He picked up a glass of water on his desk, and took a gulp .Then said, "So what brings you to my neck of the woods?"

"Business."

"Terrible about Zak Olin."

"It is."

"It's what inspired my sermon for this Sunday. Love they neighbor." He reached into a bag, took out some red pistachio nuts, then offered me some. I declined.

"You know Ben Dunn?" I asked.

"Of course."

"How do you know him?"

"We met in church a couple of years ago."

"Don't you two have very different views?"

"You might say that, but it hasn't gotten in the way of our friendship."

"Creationism."

"I prefer intelligent design."

"You say potato, I say potahto. When's the last time you saw Zak Olin?"

"Probably last Sunday in church."

"Where were you on Saturday night?"

"Me? I was right here doing some work, and when I was done, I went across the hall to my quarters to go to sleep."

"Anyone see you?"

"No. My secretary Mary doesn't work on weekends. What's your interest in my schedule?"

"Just routine."

"I don't mean to be rude, Sheriff, but I've got to get back to writing my sermon. Unlike those fancy TV ministers, I don't have a big staff to help me."

"Thanks for your time, Reverend."

✗ ✗ ✗ ✗

When I stepped out of the church, I noticed Reverend Tyler's station wagon parked nearby. It was one of those old-fashioned ones with the wood design on the side. A refurbished nineteen-sixties model. It was older than a lot of his parishioners. I took out the CSU tire impression photos, and compared them to the tires on the station wagon. Bingo. The tires were worn down just like the ones in the plaster casts.

When I walked back into the squad room, Deputy Douglas gave me some papers. "Check this out," he said. "I got it off The Speak Easy website. Ben Dunn does a double with Rev.Tyler."

I looked at the paper. It read: "Tyler and Dunn Debate Intelligent Design versus Evolution. A priest and a Biology Professor engage in lively discussion on everbody's favorite hot button topics. Available for schools, business dinners, civic centers,or any venue. Sure to draw a good-sized crowd for your event. Book them now." I looked at my Deputy. "Very interesting," I said.

"I checked Rev. Tyler's financials," said Douglas, "he does pretty well with his little dog and pony show."

I looked at the numbers and whistled. "That'll keep him in wine and wafers."

"Since it's not directly tied into the church, it goes straight into his personal account."

"His tire tracks match the photos, which puts him at the crime scene, along with his pal."

"Shall we impound the car?"

"Not yet. First, I want to make sure we get all our ducks in a row. Accusing a priest of a capital crime is a serious charge. When we do, I want to be certain that we'll be able to make it stick. Right now, all we have is circumstantial evidence."

"Ninety percent of criminals are convicted on circumstantial evidence. I heard that on TV."

"So it must be true."

"How about motive?"

"We could use one. Right now all we have are tire tracks, tobacco, and food coloring."

"Food coloring?

"That's what I think puts the good reverend Tyler at the crime scene."

"Can you explain—"

"The pistachio nuts he's always eating. They're red."

"Uh," said Douglas, "about Maggie's boyfriend, Tommy. He's still cooling his heels in holding. His uncle and a female neighbor up in the woods alibi'd him."

"Cut him loose."

I sat down at my desk and wondered what would make a priest and a science teacher want to kill a farmer. I ran this over in my mind for a few minutes, but couldn't come up with anything. Then I turned to Douglas and said: "You have any ideas as to motive?"

"Maybe he gave them some bad vegetables."

"You're a big help."

"How do we know that Maggie didn't kill her Dad?"

"You mean other than any evidence that would even vaguely suggest that?"

"Yeah."

"Dump Zak Olin's LUDs and see what turns up."

Douglas got to work, as I went through some papers on my desk. A few minutes later he came over and handed me a list of Zak Olin's calls for the last two months. I looked through the list and stopped when I noticed something.

"Here," I said, pointing to one line. "A call from last Friday, from Zak Olin to Rev. Tyler."

"I wonder what that was about."

"Tyler told me he didn't know Zak well."

"A priest who lies. Go figure."

I continued looking through the list and found a call that Zak made to Ben Dunn.

"Why is Zak talking to these two?" asked Douglas.

"I think we need to speak to his daughter," I replied.

✗ ✗ ✗ ✗

Fifteen minutes later, I was sitting in the kitchen of the Miller family home, where Maggie was staying. I sat at the table, across from Maggie, watching her eat a cracker and sip a glass of orange juice.

"Did your father keep any valuables at the house?" I asked.

"My mother's jewelry. I remember he told me after she died that it would all be mine, when I grew up. I was just a little girl at the time, and I didn't really understand."

"Was there anything missing?"

"You and the Deputy said it was a crime scene, you wouldn't let me go back inside."

"Can you think of anything else of value that your father had?"

"He had an old bible."

"How old?"

"It belonged to my grandfather, my father's father. It's a King James version. I don't know how old it is."

"Was your father a religious man?"

"After my mother died he said that he didn't know what he believed."

"Yet he went to church on Sunday."

"Yes. I had the feeling that he was conflicted about that."

"Did he keep any cash in the house?"

"Not very much. I know he collected stamps. He especially liked ones that featured farming or crops."

"I think we should go back to the house now, and you can check to see if anything's missing."

Maggie and I went outside. Deputy Douglas was waiting in his car. I had Maggie get into the front seat of mine, and we drove out to the Olin farm. Douglas followed us in his car. When we got there, I took the police seal off the door, and had Maggie go through the house. After a few minutes she reported back that nothing seemed to be missing. Maggie and I sat down on chairs in the den, as Douglas sat on a chair facing us. I scratched my head.

"What was your father's state of mind the week before you left to stay with your friend?" I asked.

"He seemed distant, like he was in a daze."

"A daze."

"When I asked him if he felt okay, he said he was fine, but he looked like he was lost in thought. This went on for days. It seemed very odd to me."

"How so?"

"Well, only the week before that he was very excited about growing carrots, peas, and lettuce on the new land he'd bought adjoining ours."

"The widow's land."

"Yes. He was so happy about buying it, and then, a few days later, he was quiet and distant. If there was a reason, I couldn't figure out what it was. He was just starting to clear the land (the old lady let it get overgrown with weeds), when he stopped. Then he collected some wood and built a little tool shed. He said he wanted to go in there to think. He wanted to be left alone. One time I peeked my head in there, and he had a fit."

"What's in the shed?"

"Nothing's in there. It's a lean-to, made out of two by fours. He put a chair in there and a box he used as a table. "

I asked Deputy Douglas to take Maggie back to her friend's house and stood on the porch, watching his car drive away and vanish into the distance. For a few minutes I stared off into the darkness wondering what to do. I had means and opportunity, but what was the motive?

I stepped off the porch, went to my car, got out my flashlight, and started walking into the field. It was easy to see the demarcation between the two properties. Olin's field was filled with neat furrows, whereas the old lady's was, as Maggie had said, mostly overgrown with weeds and vines. Not too far onto her property I saw the little shed. It was impossible to miss, as it was the only free standing structure around. Maggie had described it accurately. It wasn't too much bigger than an outhouse. There was a padlock on the door. Considering the fact that the shed looked like if you blew on it hard enough it would fall down, the idea of putting a lock on it seemed ridiculous.

I took out my Swiss army knife and pried the screws out that held the latch and lock. Then I opened the door and stepped inside the shed. Maggie was right, all that was inside was a chair, and an empty wooden box. A shovel was leaning against a wall.

The man wanted a place where could go to be alone, so he could think. That seemed reasonable. Thoreau had Walden Pond, Zak Olin had a shed. On the floor was a blue throw rug that covered most of the wood. I sat down on the chair. There was something very spiritual about farming to begin with. It was primal, as old as civilization. Tied to the seasons. Birth, life, death.

I looked at the rug on the floor and saw a couple of small bumps. I flipped the rug over and saw that they were caused by hinges from a trap door. There was a flat handle on the door. I pulled open the door and shined my flashlight into the dark hole. It smelled of manure. Why would a farmer dig a hole on his property? A well? Some kind of irrigation canal? And why put a tool shed on top of it?

I noticed a rope that was attached to some nails under the shack. I thought of Alice going down the rabbit hole. Then I picked up the rope and slid into the opening. For a few seconds all I saw was darkness and dirt, then I gently dropped to the ground below. I stood up and moved the flashlight around and saw that I was in a vast cave. There were clay pots of all sizes, statues of beautiful women in togas, gold encrusted boxes, and on the walls were what looked like some kind of elaborate hieroglyphics. They didn't look like any of the ones I'd ever seen in photographs, or in museums.

Each was more like a page with panels, not unlike a comic book. They seemed to tell a story with pictures. They looked like they were in a sequence and drawn more realistically than most I'd seen in museums. People in silver costumes, posing, pointing, climbing. They seemed to "read" from left to right. I moved left, trying to get to the beginning. I walked till I came to what appeared to be the first panel. And then I saw it. Drawings of what were unmistakably saucer-shaped spaceships. They weren't stylized. They were drawn realistically; not open to interpretation. They were ships with people walking into them. In the backgrounds were what could only be buildings. Tall glass towers, a whole city of them.

The next panel showed the people in the ships, in space, surrounded by stars and planets. The one after that showed the ships approaching a planet that, judging by the land masses, was clearly earth. The ships landed and the people got out. They were alone on a vast empty planet. They changed out of their silver clothes, built huts. The spaceships left. Then the people built towns that looked like ancient settlements; then cities that resembled Mesopotamia, Babylon, Athens, and Rome.

I went back to the rope and pulled myself up toward the tool shed. When I got into the shed I closed the trap door and pulled the rug over it. Then I opened the tool shed door and stepped outside. Standing in front of me was Ben Dunn and Reverend Tyler. Dunn was pointing a gun at me.

"Hands up, Sheriff. Don't even think about going for your gun or I'll use mine."

I put my hands up. Tyler came over to me and pulled my gun out of its holster, then went back to Dunn.

"What's this all about?" I asked.

"Don't insult our intelligence, Sheriff," said Dunn, "we know you've seen it."

"Put down your gun," I said, "we can talk about this."

"There's nothing to talk about."

"Reverend, I said, "you're a man of God, how can you—"

"God helps those who help themselves," said Tyler.

"Look," I said, "let's settle this peacefully."

"Sorry, Sheriff," said Dunn, "this is bigger than all of us. Now please stand over there, away from the shed."

I moved to the side of the shed, as Dunn gave Rev. Tyler the gun. Tyler then took my gun, and put it into the waist band of his pants.

"You make a move, Sheriff, and the Reverend will shoot you," said Dunn. "I'll be gone for a few minutes. Don't do anything foolish."

Dunn picked up a shopping bag, went into the shed, and closed the door. I turned to Rev. Tyler.

"Is this really worth going to prison for?" I asked.

"I don't care to engage you in a discussion, Sheriff."

"Give me the gun."

"No."

"I can understand Dunn, he's just a teacher, but you, you're someone who a lot of people in this town believe in. You're a role model."

"It had to be taken care of."

"Is that what you call murdering a man in cold blood? What happened to, Thou Shalt Not Kill?"

"You don't understand."

"Try me."

"It's about faith."

"No, it's about preserving your own beliefs. It's about not liking the facts you've found, then killing to cover them up."

"It's not like that."

"It's exactly like that. It's also about keeping the little sideshow you have with Dunn going."

"No."

"If the world were aware of what was under that tool shed…."

"Shut up!"

"And if I don't, you'll kill me, too?

"We didn't want to kill Zak Olin, it just happened."

"You've said enough," said Dunn, as he stepped out of the shed. He went over to Rev. Tyler, took back his gun and pointed it at me, as Tyler took out my gun and did the same. "Now, let's start walking," said Dunn.

We moved in the direction of Olin's house, as I said, "What happens now?"

"None of your business," said Dunn.

Then we turned and walked to an area just off the road, where I saw Dunn's car parked behind some bushes. Dunn directed me to get into the back seat. Tyler sat next to me, pointing my own gun at me, while Dunn got behind the wheel. He started the engine and drove onto the road. A minute went by and I saw Dunn reach over to a paper bag that was next to him on the passenger seat, pull out a small device about the size of cell phone, and press a button on it. Then, outside, in the distance, there was a huge booming sound; and the fields near Zack Olin's house lit up like the fourth of July. The ground shook.

I punched Tyler in the jaw and grabbed my gun. I saw Dunn go for his.

"You touch your gun and I'll kill you," I said.

Dunn stepped on the gas, pushing me backward, but I held onto my gun tightly.

"Stop the car," I said.

Dunn pulled it over to the side of the road.

"Now get out, both of you," I said. They got out. " Keep your hands in the air where I can see them." I reached for my cell phone.

⚡ ⚡ ⚡ ⚡

A few minutes later, half the county was there. The fire department, three volunteer units from nearby towns, and more police vehicles than I could count. It took hours to bring the fire under control. And then the field looked like a smoldering war zone, gutted with craters.

I brought my two prisoners back to the squad room, booked them for murder, and placed them in lock-up. The next day, with a promise of leniency, Tyler ratted on his friend Dunn, saying that it was all Dunn's idea. Left out of Tyler's confession was any mention of their archeological discovery. In Tyler's newly revised version, he and Dunn were only after Zak Olin's stamp collection, in order to pay off gambling debts. The explosion was now an accident caused by Dunn. I was all too happy to endorse Tyler's story, as any other possible explanation, had been reduced to dust by the explosion.

A couple of days later, after all the TV cameras and reporters went home and things returned to some version of what passed for normal, my Deputy took me aside and asked me what really happened.

"There seems to be something missing in the official explanation," he said.

"This is strictly off the record. A month ago, Zak Olin bought fifteen acres of land adjoining his property from his elderly widowed neighbor. She'd never developed the land. Shortly after he acquired it with the intention to farm it, he found something very unusual."

"What?"

"An archeological find that could have altered mankind's views of history, science, and religion forever. It was a cave containing ancient pictures and hieroglyphics that recorded the human race's migration from another planet to this one."

"You're kidding."

"We have one murder and a crater the size of a shopping mall. Do I look like I'm kidding? The hieroglyphics tell the story of an earth without any native people. And then being colonized by humans from another world. By extrapolation, there was no evolution and no creationism. Men and women appeared on this planet in one day from someplace else. The earth was seeded by aliens and we, that is, all of us, are their descendants. All of history would be rewritten, and oh, yeah, Dunn and Tyler would also be out of a job."

"How do you know this cave was real and not just some kind of hoax?"

"I suppose I don't, and I'll never know for sure. But Tyler and Dunn thought it was real, or maybe they just couldn't take the chance. But I do know that there are many precedents for finding ancient artifacts in America."

"You mean like Viking runestones in Maine?"

"That's just the tip of the iceberg. There are ancient dolmen, or standing stones, not unlike Stonehenge, only smaller, in New England. So called 'root cellars' in Connecticut, that just happen to work like ancient calendars; there are the mound builders in Ohio and reports of Egyptian artifacts from antiquity that have been found all over America. Many believe that the Grand Canyon was once part of an inland sea."

"How do you know all this?"

"The internet," I said, smiling.

"Okay, let's say, for the sake of argument, that what they found was real, or at least they believed it to be real."

"Zak Olin made the discovery, then he called Reverend Tyler to tell him about it. Tyler called his friend, Ben Dunn. Both of them went over to Olin's to see what he'd found. Once they saw it, they realized the significance immediately, and tried to talk Olin out of going public with it. More than likely, they offered to pay him off to keep quiet. But Olin wasn't about to take hush money, and he wasn't going away. He was, no doubt, going to make a public announcement. This would have been potentially bigger than the Dead Sea scrolls, and the La Croix caves in France put together. The ensuing media storm might have gone on for years. This was something Dunn and Tyler could not allow. In a fit of panic and rage, Dunn went into the kitchen, got a frying pan, and bashed Olin's head in. Then he and Tyler fled the scene."

"Wow."

"But there was still the matter of destroying the cave. They couldn't take the chance that someone else might stumble upon it, which, in fact, is just what I did. Dunn had already set the stage with bags of fertilizer, the choice of many of our homegrown terrorists. Just after I got there, he was about to set a remote-controlled timer, which he did, while I waited with Tyler pointing his gun at me. In any case, all that Zak Olin discovered is now a pile of dirt."

"Their speaking engagements and their beliefs are now, once again, safe from the truth."

"I'm not sure how much public speaking they'll be doing in prison."

I looked at my Deputy and said, "We never had this conversation."

"What conversation?" he replied.

A few nights later, I found myself unable to sleep. I went outside and stood on my porch. The sky was dark and filled with thousands of stars. They were the same stars I'd seen since I was a boy, only now, somehow, they all looked different. After a while, I went back inside, got into bed, and eventually fell asleep.

✗

THE CURIOUS CASE OF ARTHUR CONAN DOYLE

by Sherlock Holmes, Consulting Detective

AS TOLD BY

Gary Lovisi

I, Sherlock Holmes, take up my pen in firm resolve to put to paper some items that have concerned me of late, and which I feel need to be aired. The topic concerns the relationship with Mr. Arthur Conan Doyle. Doyle surely is a complicated man, much like myself, so I do understand the type, and for that reason I have over the years allowed him certain liberties with Watson's writings and words detailing my life and work. However, now, since he has prompted Watson to bring me back to life again—although with the utmost reluctance—the problem has come to a head and I can remain silent no longer. I feel I must put these words to paper for posterity.

After much thought and reflection, I have come to the truth of the matter between us, and that is, I have been abominably treated by Mr. Doyle over the many years of my long career and our association. While I am naturally thankful for his work as literary agent and of ensuring my story be told—through the goodly Watson—there is a deeper aspect to our relationship that has been left unspoken, until now.

I feel I have been ill-treated by Mr. Doyle. First he watched as Watson placed me in all types of dangerous situations and he gave me every manner of seemingly impossible crime to solve. And I did! I solved them all! Did I ever complain? I even cherished the challenges. However, while all this was going on he spoke a never-ending barrage of harsh words about me over a period of many years—he even said he despised me! I who never said an ill word about him! Then the worst insult of all—he finally suggested that Watson kill me! However, even in death Doyle's animus to me did not abate, as he often spoke harshly about me *after* my demise.

This is a problem that has been building up between us for a long time now and it peaked my curiosity upon my resurrection not long after Watson brought me back to life. At the time Doyle's words shocked me greatly as I noticed how he often spoke of how deeply he hated me—he even said he "despised" me. Even more shocking, he was quite open about his negative feelings towards me—while in the same breath he spoke glowingly of his own historical novels and their characters—Loring of *The White Company*, or *Michah Clarke*. As if they were in the same category as myself. Was he serious?

Doyle's vast calumny against me only grew over the years and I could not understand it. It hurt me deeply. After all he had a hand in creating me—I did not create him! Or did I! I sometimes wonder? My cases certainly did make his writing career. Some might even say that Sherlock Holmes was the creator of Mr. Doyle—the author!

When Doyle desired that I was killed off at the height of my career I could hardly believe it. How could he want such a thing? I can only believe it was an effort by him to stifle my great success. If you recall, I had just then put a stop to Professor Moriarty and his vast criminal organization, and in doing so I was at the height of my power and success. I tell you in all truth this was a terrible shock to me, a massive blow, to discover Doyle had actually wanted me killed off. Why did he want it? Then Doyle had me brought back years later, but only after much pressure from the public and because as Watson's agent he was paid more than he had ever been paid before for a new story about me. *Me!* Sherlock Holmes! Seems no one was interested very much in anything else Doyle was writing. I believe the only reason for his behavior was because he was jealous of me, and of my growing fame—which was then eclipsing his own. Everyone knew the name Sherlock Holmes—and while Doyle was a popular and talented author in his own right—I do give him credit for that—he was certainly no Sherlock Holmes!

Even in 1893 at the time of my death he was still speaking out against me—making comments on how he hated Sherlock Holmes—and me being recently deceased at the time. Not very nice to speak so harshly of the dead, Mr. Doyle. In fact, being such a serious proponent of spiritualism, and desiring to communicate with the souls of the departed who reside in the spirit world, one would think he would speak kinder words about me upon my demise. He did not. He never even made an attempt to contact me in his precious spirit realm. Even my death did not stop him from viciously maligning me and my memory.

I had thought Moriarty my greatest enemy—but it turned out to be my greatest enemy was Arthur Conan Doyle!

In all truth I tell you it was never I who did him any wrong. I have done nothing other than benefit the man, improving his literary standing with the public as well as his financial fortunes. In fact, it was he who has done me a grievous wrong and harm. Now I seek to get to the nub of the matter and solve this curious case for some explanation of his behavior towards me. I am sad to say that it has been rather despicable.

As the scoundrel once told a friend about me—after I was killed off in "The Final Problem": "I couldn't revive him if I would, at least not for years, for I have had such an overdose of him that I feel towards him as I do towards *pate de foie gras*, of which I once ate too much, so that the name of it gives me a sickly feeling to this day."

Well, I am afraid the feeling is now quite mutual. I am tired of hearing about Doyle too now, please do not mention him around me.

Why, you might ask, would Doyle hold such distain for me? I have looked into the matter and come up with an interesting theory, based upon fact and evidence, as is my method. I believe there is more to this strange case than meets the eye, my friends. That is because, I myself was based upon a real person, Dr. Joseph Bell. Bell was Doyle's teacher at university and Doyle would become his personal clerk, and no doubt he greatly admired Bell. Doyle admired Bell so much that he had Watson use him as the basis for my very own persona. In fact, in 1892 Doyle wrote to his mentor admitting as much, saying, "It is certainly to you that I owe Sherlock Holmes…I do not think that his analytical work is in the least an exaggeration of some effects which I have seen you produce in the out-patient ward."

Now, Dr. Bell was a proper Victorian, and thought to be, by Doyle, rather cold and emotionless. Of course Bell was anything but cold or emotionless. Nevertheless, Doyle was fascinated by him—perhaps even obsessed?—for it is well documented that he craved a closer friendship with Bell, affection he needed and missed but never received from his own father. Doyle's father was an artist and quite creative but he was emotionally unstable and eventually had to be institutionalized. As I have often stated, art in the blood can make for some rather strange consequences.

Be that as it may, taking into account what I know, I believe Doyle was in fact jealous of Dr. Bell, and while he based some of my persona and talents upon Bell, he held a deep-rooted animosity towards him—which also transferred towards me. Doyle was jealous of Joe Bell—and Doyle as a result—became jealous of me, Sherlock Holmes. Logic and deduction lead me to believe no other conclusion is possible.

Let us set the record straight here. It is clear that Doyle thought me unworthy of his great literary talents, but it was I, Sherlock Holmes, and no other, who brought Doyle vast wealth and fame. It was I, who allowed him the financial basis to write all his other writings—many of which I am not enamored with. Most of which did not sell well, or only sold at all because they were written by the man who was so closely associated with the great Sherlock Holmes stories. It was I who kept Doyle in the public light and ensured his work appeared in many periodicals. My cases were the impetus for readers to ask for him to write his own books, to make speeches and be invited to attend lavish parties and social events. It may seem harsh to say, but the evidence is undeniable. I have been greatly wronged by Mr. Doyle and now seek satisfaction.

As a result, I can only declare that regarding the curious case of Arthur Conan Doyle—evidence shows that he has treated me abominably. Quite frankly, I have come to the conclusion that rather than *I* not being worthy of Doyle—Doyle does not deserve *me!*

Gary Lovisi is an MWA Edgar-nominated author for Best Short Story for his Sherlock Holmes pastiche "The Adventure of The Missing Detective." He is a Holmes fan and collector who writes various articles and short stories of, and about, The Great Detective, some of which have appeared in this magazine. He is the editor of *Paperback Parade*, and of the recent Sherlock Holmes anthology, *The Great Detective: His Further Adventures* (Wildside Press). His forthcoming book *The Third Secret Adventures of Sherlock Holmes* (Ramble House) will collect four pastiches for the first time in book form. You can find out more about him, and his work, at his website: www.gryphonbooks.com.

THE DAYTIME SERIAL KILLER

Dan Andriacco

Even before Brock McKenna fully opened the apartment door, a look of recognition registered upon his once-handsome face.

"Oh, it's you," he said in a voice dripping with contempt. "Somehow I had a feeling it would be. Well, come in and let's get this over with. I'm not surprised you're…hey, what are you doing with that gun? Take it easy now, that thing could blow a hole —"

Three shots rang out in rapid fire. McKenna staggered back, stumbled against a love seat and fell to the floor. After that he didn't move.

A man in his later years and a pretty young woman watched the unfolding drama on a TV monitor.

"This has been fascinating to watch from here in here," commented Lafcadio Figg. A stocky man with gray chin-length hair and mutton-chop whiskers, he wore his coat over his shoulders like a cape. "So who killed the nefarious Brock McKenna?"

"I don't know, Professor," Gillian Burke said. With ash-blond hair and a boyish figure, she looked even younger than her twenty-seven years. "That's not revealed in the scripts we've shot so far. I bet Eric doesn't even know— Eric Lord, who plays Brock McKenna. Come on, we're off the air now. Let's ask him."

They left the control booth and soon found themselves in the room they had been watching, one familiar to veteran fans of the long-running soap opera, "Tomorrow is Another Day." It felt strange to Figg, as if he had walked into a film and become one of the characters.

"We built some amazing sets at school, but this one is in a different league," he told Gillian. "I could almost believe we're in a real apartment."

"The details have to be right. Brock McKenna does a lot of his naughty romancing in this apartment. Right, Eric? Eric!"

As Gillian stared down at the motionless form, Figg noticed for the first time that the actor hadn't changed his position since he'd fallen to the floor several minutes earlier.

With some difficulty because of his bulk and age, Figg knelt down for a closer look.

"Did he hit his head when he fell?" Gillian asked.

Figg shook his hairy head. "No, it's not that, my dear. There's blood oozing out of Mr. Lord's chest. I think he's dead."

✗ ✗ ✗ ✗

Lt. Al Kowalski, NYPD, knew that he looked like a recruiting poster for the Marines—crew cut, six-four, muscular build. Sometimes that was an advantage, but not when he was trying to set witnesses at ease. He tried to compensate with a friendly manner. He started by introducing himself and his sergeant, Rico Carlotta, to the old guy and the actress.

"Naturally, we have to ask you a few questions since you were the first to realize that the deceased had actually been killed. Your producer said we could talk here without being interrupted."

Kowalski's mind told him that he was on a TV set, but his eyes said otherwise. The murder scene looked a lot like his uncle's apartment in Minneapolis, but without the photos of kids and old people over the brick mantelpiece of the gas fireplace. Apparently Brock McKenna hadn't been much of family man.

"I hope we can help, Lieutenant, but I don't see how," the actress said.

"But who are you, really?" Carlotta asked. "Raven or Kristen?"

Kowalski regarded the younger cop with irritation. His dark-haired subordinate was a good officer, but inclined to lose focus. He was also about fifteen pounds overweight; Kowalski made a mental note to talk to him about that.

"I'm both, Sergeant," Gillian said with a chuckle. "And neither, of course."

Kowalski was lost. "Isn't your name Gillian Burke?"

"That's right, Lieutenant. But I play two parts on 'Tomorrow is Another Day.' In my natural hair, I'm the heroine, Kristen Calloway Nicholas. When I wear a black wig, I'm that awful tramp Raven McKenna. They're twins, you see, but Raven was stolen away from the hospital by her unwed father, Brock McKenna, shortly after she was born. They only returned to the town of River Bend about a year and a half ago."

"Brock is romancing Myrna Calloway, Kristen and Raven," Carlotta said. "But he's also fooling around with Myrna's youngest child, Fane Calloway. And Raven stole Kristen's husband, Quint Nicholas. You're rotten, Raven, just like your father."

"Sergeant!"

"Sorry, Lieutenant. I got carried away." Carlotta looked shamefaced. "I'm kind of into the show. I DVR it."

Gillian Burke smiled. Kowalski couldn't help noticing how fresh and innocent she looked. "That's quite all right. We daytime serial actors are used to being mistaken for the characters we play. It's kind of a compliment. Our fans scold us, root for us and warn us when our lovers are cheating on us. Good girls get proposals and bad girls get propositions. With the two roles I play, I get both."

Actors! Kowalski thought. "Thanks for clearing that up. Unlike my sergeant"—he shot darts at Carlotta—"I don't watch much TV. Now then…" He turned to the fourth person in the room. "You're Professor Lafcadio Figg, right?"

Figg bowed in a courtly fashion. "At your service, Lieutenant."

"I understand that you're a visitor to the program. What brings you here?"

"Many years ago, when Miss Burke's last name was Krauthammer and I taught drama at the School for Creative and Performing Arts in Cincinnati, she was a student of mine. I don't get to New York very often, so when I found myself here to discuss a textbook project with a publisher, I resolved to visit one of my more successful pupils. Frankly, I am still shocked by having witnessed the tragic accident."

"Accident?" Kowalski shook his head. "The death of Eric Lord was no accident. It was cold-blooded murder."

Gillian Burke sucked in her breath. Figg put his arm around her in a paternal way.

Kowalski studied the faces of the two witnesses, trying to figure out if they were really as surprised as they looked. But he quickly gave that up as almost hopeless. The Burke woman was a professional actress. She lied for a living. And Figg had a theatrical connection, too. If he'd taught drama, he'd probably acted as well. How could he tell whether they were giving him the straight goods or putting on a show? He had no particular reason to be suspicious of them, but also no reason not to be.

"What happened?" Gillian asked.

"Murder by proxy, you might say. Somebody replaced the blanks in the prop gun with live bullets. A prop woman—Agnes Reis, her name is—pulled the trigger. She's in the hospital now, a basket case. But the real killer is whoever fiddled with that gun."

Gillian Burke shook her head. "Poor Agnes. But who…" She didn't finish the rhetorical question.

"At this stage, everybody's a suspect." Technically, that was true. In reality, Kowalski figured the killer had to be someone who knew that the script called for the shooting of Brock McKenna, which presumably was a relatively small circle of people. Kowalski would get the list from the producer. But the witnesses didn't have to know that. "You and Mr. Figg were the first ones on the scene after the shooting. Did you touch anything?"

"Of course not," Figg said while Gillian shook her head. "Anybody who's ever seen 'CSI' knows better."

"Ms. Burke, you're familiar with the set where the murder took place. Did you see anything unusual or out of order?"

"I don't think so," Gillian said. "But if the killer simply switched bullets and left it to Agnes to do his dirty work, what would there be to see?"

"Probably nothing," Kowalski conceded. *She's a smart one*, he thought. "But a careful killer might hang around to make sure that things went according to plan—or maybe he'd be sure to be absent when the gun was fired. Did you see anybody or anything that shouldn't have been there? Or was there anyone *not* there who should have been?"

Gillian appeared to give that a hard think. She even closed her eyes. "No," she said when she opened them again. "I was showing the set to Professor Figg right after the end of the episode when we realized that Eric wasn't moving. I think I would have noticed then if anything was different."

"All right." Kowalski ran a hand through his crew cut. He asked the duo several other questions about where they had been and what they had seen before the shooting, all leading to nothing. That was par for the course at this stage. "Has anything unusual been going on around here lately—behind the scenes stuff?"

Kowalski expected her answer to be more of the same, but Gillian served up a surprise. "There was one strange thing. The digital tape of today's show went missing four days ago. That's why we broadcast the show live today for the first time anybody can remember. Larry Chaney—our producer—said it would cost too much to re-tape."

The news hit Kowalski like a sock in the gut. If this was the second time through the script, then probably a lot more people knew about the shooting of Eric Lord's character than just the script writer, the producer and anybody they told. His dream of a short list of suspects had just died a wretched death. Anybody connected with this godforsaken soap opera could have substituted the bullets in the prop gun!

He was still processing that when somebody's grandma came through the door of the set, panting as though she'd just run a half-marathon. But she had a smile on her face.

"Kristen! I just heard the news about Brock being shot!"

The woman was plump and short with page-boy style gray hair in disarray. She wore a heavy red sweater with a black leather shoulder bag slung over it. Her lipstick application didn't quite match her lips. Kowalski figured her age at late sixties, but he wasn't about to give her a senior citizen's discount on police procedure. He addressed her sternly:

"This is a private police interview, Ms.—"

"Lieutenant, this is Maggie Dunbar, long-time editor of *Soap Opera Secrets* magazine and website," Gillian said. "She knows every daytime serial on the air as if she were living it herself. Here at 'Tomorrow is Another Day' she's practically a member of the cast. Maggie, these gentlemen are policemen investigating the murder."

"You're pretty cheerful for somebody who just heard about a murder," Carlotta observed, eying the newcomer with ill-concealed suspicion.

"And why shouldn't I be, young man? I shall shed no crocodile tears for Brock McKenna. With him out of the way, Fane will go back to Luke Savage, her old boyfriend, and Myrna will return to her husband, Derek. Derek's heading back to town, you know. He's had amnesia for fifteen years, but he's cured now. If that wicked Raven would leave Quint alone, then all would be well in River Bend. But I suppose that's too much to ask."

Nothing in his course work at the John Jay College of Criminal Justice or his fourteen years on the force prepared Kowalski for all that bilge. Maggie Dunbar obviously didn't know that Eric Lord was really dead. Maybe that was just as well. It would make it easier to get rid of her. How had a magazine editor wound up on the murder scene in the first place?

Gillian Burke opened her mouth as if to enlighten the older woman, but Kowalski cut her off. "Rico, show Ms. Dunbar out."

From the outraged look on Dunbar's face, he feared she was going to punch him or slug him with her shoulder bag. "You can't treat the press like this!"

"Write your Congressman."

She continued protesting as Carlotta gently led her out the door.

"Maggie gets a little carried away sometimes," Gillian said. Before Kowalski could make an appropriately acid comment, Carlotta returned with a thoughtful expression on his face.

"Actually, Ms. Dunbar may be on to something," he said. "Suppose all that stuff does happen because Brock McKenna has to be written out of the storyline. Maybe there's a motive there—like, for instance, an actor who wanted to fatten up his part by taking out his character's romantic rival."

Kowalski raised his sandy eyebrows. The idea wasn't completely nuts— just wrong. "You get full points for ingenuity, Rico, but you forgot something: Brock McKenna was out of the program after this episode, anyway. He's dead."

Carlotta shook his head. "Maybe not, Lieutenant. There are a lot of shootings, poisonings, beatings, strangling and whatnot on these shows, but sometimes the victims recover. Dr. Sylvia Harding on 'Promise of Tomorrow' has been shot four times and stabbed once."

Restraining the impulse to comment on the younger man's extensive knowledge of daytime drama, Kowalski turned to Gillian. "Sergeant Carlotta raises an interesting point, Ms. Burke. Not being a soap opera connoisseur, that didn't occur to me. Was Brock McKenna going to die or recover?"

The actress shrugged. "That information is above my pay grade. All I can tell you is that Brock is still in the hospital in the episodes we've taped so far, but we're only a couple of weeks ahead of the air date. The technicians went on strike last fall and we're not back to our usual one-month lead time yet."

"Who would know what's going to happen to the character farther on?"

"Ask our producer, Larry Chaney."

✗   ✗   ✗   ✗

They found Chaney de-stressing at the network's gym. He was a medium-build guy in black horn-rim glasses and a goatee streaked with gray. He lifted fifty-pound free-weights in each hand as he spoke to the detective through clenched teeth. His Sergeant Pepper T-shirt was stained with sweat.

"We can understand that you're upset, Mr. Chaney —"

"Upset? Lieutenant, this is like a death in the family. And it's murder. I get ulcers just thinking about the headlines in *The New York Post*. Not to mention what the other networks will do with it on their evening news."

Not a word of grief about Eric Lord, Kowalski noted. "Sergeant Carlotta and I just have a few questions for you. First of all, where is the storyline of 'Tomorrow is Another Day' going?"

"Which one? Do you realize how many intertwined storylines a soap has?"

Carlotta cleared his throat. "What the Lieutenant really wants to know is, what happens to Brock McKenna next? Is he history or not?"

Cheney set the weights down and began wiping his face with a towel. "Well, he isn't dead yet. For several weeks he's going to have an out-of-body experience while Detective Hopper investigates the shooting. Hopper has already been working with the narcs investigating rumors about Brock's nightclub."

Carlotta nodded knowingly. "Everybody in River Bend knows that a Columbian drug cartel put up the money for Brock to buy the club."

"So naturally they're hot suspects in the shooting," Chaney said.

"But I bet they didn't do it."

"No, Sergeant. They didn't. Keep this under your hat, but Myrna did it. Last week she caught Brock in bed with Fane. He should have known it's poison to fool around with a mother and her daughter at the same time."

Kowalski's head was swimming. "You still haven't told me whether the Brock McKenna character was going to be going to be written out of the show."

"Oh. Well, that hasn't been decided yet. It probably would have depended on how Eric's contract negotiations went. But maybe not. If we got a lot of 'bring back Brock' activity on social media and Eric wanted too much money, we could always hire a new Brock McKenna. We've done it before. It might even improve ratings."

Ratings? Kowalski's antennae went up. "You said yourself the murder is going to get a lot of media coverage. That'll boost your ratings sky-high, won't it?"

Chaney glared at Kowalski. Then, with a sudden motion, he threw himself down on a mat and starting doing push-ups. "What are you trying to imply, Lieutenant?" He pushed out between pushes.

"I didn't imply anything. I was just making an observation. I would be implying something if I said that Eric Lord's spectacular demise seemed to be a good thing for the show, assuming your sponsor cares about ratings."

"Our ratings are already terrific, thank you. We've been the top-rated soap for the past five years. And we collected a handful of daytime Emmys in the same period—one of which went to Eric. Any other questions?"

"A few. For instance, I wanted to ask you about the theft of the digital tape for today's episode."

Chaney sat, his legs crossed, and wiped himself again. "You heard about that, huh? What a pain! You should have been backstage five minutes before the show started today. Panic City! There are people in the cast who'd never acted in a live performance before, not even in high school. But I wasn't about to re-tape. That would have cost hundreds of thousands of dollars. Besides, we got a nice little publicity bump from going live for the first time since 1968. Maggie Dunbar wrote three stories about it for the *Soap Opera Secrets* website. Page Six gave it a little virtual ink, too."

In other words, today's special on-air performance of the soap was widely known in advance among people who paid attention to such things. Kowalski made a mental note of that.

"Any idea who took the tape?" Carlotta asked. "Or why?"

Chaney shook his head vigorously. "Your guess is as good as mine."

"Maybe even better," Kowalski said. "I've been kicking around a little idea." Actually, it had just come to him. "When did members of the cast know that the Brock McKenna character was going to be shot?"

"Not until scripts went out a few days before the taping. We try to keep a lid on big plot developments as long as we can." That tracked with the impression Gillian Burke had given. "But once the cameras rolled on the shooting scene, everybody connected with the show knew."

"So if somebody wanted to do away with Eric Lord in a particularly cute way," Carlotta said, "he could have stolen the tape of the show and forced you to do it over again—this time with real bullets in the gun. Is that what you're thinking, Lieutenant?"

Kowalski nodded. "It would explain the theft of the tape. Who had access to both the prop gun and the tape, Mr. Chaney?"

"Hell, dozens of people are running around the studio with nobody paying attention to them—actors, camera people, costume and set designers, wardrobe mistresses, make-up artists, sound and lighting technicians. It's a zoo."

"Still, we'll have to talk to all of them. I'd like to set up headquarters in your office where I can meet with them one at a time without some old lady barging in."

"Fine. I'll have coffee sent in for you."

"Thanks. Rico, poke around the sets of 'Tomorrow is Another Day' and the offices and dressing rooms of the people who work on it. If you find anybody who doesn't belong—*anybody*—bring him in. We've already run into a retired teacher and a magazine editor acting like they own the place. Lord knows who else might be lurking around—maybe our killer."

✗ ✗ ✗ ✗

"Your name is Travis Kemp and you play Quint Nichols, Kristen's former husband. Do I have all that right?"

"That's it, Lieutenant. But don't blame me for fooling around with Raven. She tricked me into it by wearing a wig and dressing like Kristen. Then she blackmailed me into a real affair. When I thought she had AIDS, naturally the gentlemanly thing toward Kristen…"

Kowalski's head hurt. "Let's just stick to the murder and the leave the plot twists to people who care. Tell me about Eric Lord."

Kemp, in his mid-twenties with wavy brown hair like a Ken doll, shrugged. "What's to tell? He was a bully, a prima donna and what they used to call a skirt chaser when he was young, which was several decades ago."

"You didn't like him?"

"Nobody did."

"You mean he never caught any of those skirts he was chasing?"

"I wouldn't go that far. His suave older man routine appealed to a certain type of impressionistic young woman. But his batting average wasn't what I'd call major league."

Kowalski hated sports metaphors. He asked Kemp if there were any jealous boyfriends, jealous ex-flames, anybody who might have the reason to kill Lord. The actor professed to know of none. "I think the only deep emotion Eric generated was contempt, not real hatred."

Moving on, Kowalski asked, "Did you see anything out of the ordinary on the set today?"

"I wasn't even in today's taping or the live episode that followed. I just dropped by a half-hour ago to pick up a sport coat I left in my dressing room. Larry Chaney saw me and told me to come in here."

Just as Kowalski was thinking how convenient it was for Kemp that he wasn't in the building at the time of the murder—or so he said—there was a knock on the door.

"Can I come in Lieutenant?" A tall African-American officer stuck his head in the room.

"You're already in, Officer Jackson. But that's okay. Mr. Kemp is just leaving. Call me if you remember anything important, Mr. Kemp."

"Count on it."

Kemp fled, as if he were afraid the lieutenant would change his mind. As he went out the door, Jackson came in, carrying what seemed to be a large oil portrait of an older man with hair too full and dark to be real.

"Isn't that a painting of the dead man?" Kowalski asked.

"It's actually a photograph printed on canvas to look like a painting, Lieutenant. But it is the vic. And look at this."

Jackson pointed to a series of slash marks across the painted face of the late Eric Lord, ripping through a sardonic smile. "Somebody really had it in for that guy."

"Where did you find it?"

"In a corner of the prop room."

"Good work, Jumal." Kowalski was always careful to praise his men when they deserved it, especially those who were being unfairly held back from promotion right now because of budget cuts in the department. "Have it dusted for prints and let me know what turns up."

✗ ✗ ✗ ✗

"Ms. Rivers, I don't watch soap operas, but I'll never forget you in *Cross of Gold.*"

"How very sweet of you to say so, Lieutenant."

She was petite, smaller than she looked on the big screen. But well into her seventh decade, her figure was still perfect and her face would have made a statue of a Greek goddess weep with envy. Kowalski couldn't believe he was actually talking to Constance Rivers, star of a dozen classic films and winner of multiple Oscars. "I fell in love with you in that movie, just like every other male. I was twelve years old when I first saw it." He paused. How to put this? "No offense, ma'am, but what happened?"

"To my career, you mean?" Constance Rivers sighed. "A lot of people wonder that, although few have the courage to say so. I got older, that's all. Good film roles aren't so easy to come by for a woman my age. Directors would rather have 'a young Constance Rivers,' whoever that is this year. At least I'm working. And I rather like playing Myrna Calloway. She's a strong-willed woman and a bit younger than I am. But I suppose it's Eric Lord you want to talk about."

Embarrassed that the witness had to remind him of that, Kowalski said, "Did you know him well?"

"Well enough. I was married to him for three years."

"Oh. I didn't know."

"He was one of my less famous husbands."

"I hear he was quite the ladies man."

"He thought so. Eric's wish list was always longer than his resumé when it came to women. He liked young vulnerable actresses. Unfortunately for him, the young ones aren't so vulnerable these days and the vulnerable ones aren't so young. But that didn't stop him from trying hard."

Actors! "This was going on while you two were married to each other?"

"Before, during and after. Eric Lord was remarkably consistent, Lieutenant."

Kowalski never had time to get married, but he couldn't imagine any straight man cheating on Constance Rivers. "It must have been rough for you to see him on the set of the show—even do love scenes with him."

"Not at all. Eric and I have been on the best of terms ever since we divorced. I invited him to all of my subsequent weddings."

"Do you know who he was hitting on lately?"

The actress crossed her shapely legs. Kowalski thought of Sophia Loren, also still turning heads in her seventies. "I'm afraid I don't. I didn't care enough to notice or to inquire."

✗ ✗ ✗ ✗

"So you're Mindy Stark and you play the little sister on the show—Fane Calloway. Please spare me the plot synopsis—I've had enough of that."

The actress smiled. Kowalski couldn't help thinking that she was "a young Constance Rivers," another petite brunette, but this one on the south side of twenty-five. "You're probably thinking 'Tomorrow is Another Day' is not exactly Shakespeare. But have you ever actually considered the plots in Shakespeare? Or grand opera, for that matter?"

Kowalski, whose knowledge of opera was limited to what he picked up from Bug Bunny cartoons, was spared from answering by a voice shouting just outside the borrowed office. "I said I'm going in there."

The door burst open. A tall darkly handsome man in his forties barged in. He was immediately tackled to the office floor by a beefy officer. Mindy Stark screamed.

"Who the hell are you?" Kowalski demanded.

"Arthur Morgan. Get this ape off of me."

"Not until you show some manners."

"Arthur's not on the show," Mindy said. "He's my husband."

"And you're not going to give her the third degree without me."

That sounded ridiculous, uttered in a gasping voice from beneath a two hundred and fifty pound member of New York's Finest.

"Well done, Alvarez, but you can let him up now." Alvarez, who had done two tours of duty in Iraq and one in Afghanistan in his Air Force days, looked skeptical.

"What?" Kowalski said. "Don't you think I can handle him?"

Alvarez stood up without answering, pulling Morgan with him. "I'll be right outside the door if you need me, Lieutenant."

He closed the door loudly.

Kowalski gave the intruder his best drill-sergeant look. "So, Morgan, you don't want your wife to talk to me alone. Does she have something to hide?"

"You can't bully me with that tough cop talk. I used to play Bart Tolliver, the hard-hitting defense attorney on 'The Sands of Time.'"

"Funny, I was sizing you up for a different role—jealous husband. Maybe you were jealous enough to take extreme action against a guy with a reputation for being very fond of young actresses."

Morgan recoiled as if he'd been slapped. "Jealous? Art Morgan jealous of that has-been Eric Lord? Don't make me laugh. I'm insulted."

"And I resent your implication, Lieutenant," Mindy Stark said, turning red beneath her expertly applied makeup.

"But I don't hear you denying it."

"I deny it."

"The notorious womanizer Eric Lord was on the set day after day with an attractive young woman like you and he didn't make a pass?"

"Oh, he made plenty of passes, but they weren't completed passes."

Of course she would say that if she wanted to protect her husband and/ or avoid a lot of messy publicity. Kowalski figured that Morgan must be about twice his wife's age. But the victim was even older. Still, Kowalski encountered even odder triangles.

"Were you on the set today, Mr. Morgan?"

"What of it?" The actor's chiseled face was a study in pugnacity. "I like to see my wife. That's why I married her."

"Doesn't your own job keep you busy somewhere else?"

Morgan hesitated. "I'm between jobs at the moment—like a lot of people these days."

Mindy Stark took Morgan's hand. The look on her face was either sheer adoration or great acting.

There was a knock on the door. *Now what?* "What is it?" Kowalski barked.

"It's Jackson," came the muffled voice. "I've got some news."

The lieutenant turned to the couple. "You love birds can leave now, but don't leave town. I may want to talk to you later."

Morgan opened the door and the couple left without saying another word. Jackson squeezed past them, carrying the vandalized painting of Eric Lord in his gloved hands.

"Okay, what is it?" Kowalski asked.

"We got a match on some prints. They belong to an actress named Gillian Burke."

✗ ✗ ✗ ✗

Kowalski visited Gillian in her dressing room, where she'd been asked to wait in case the police wanted to talk to her again. Kowalski thought that going to her turf might lower her defenses.

"I hope this won't take too long, Lieutenant." She straightened her stockings. Her legs weren't as sculpted as those of Constance Rivers, but they had his attention. "I'm supposed to meet Professor Figg for dinner."

"I'm glad the murder hasn't put you off your feed," Kowalski said dryly.

"Oh, please don't think I'm hard! I'm still very upset. I can't get the sight of that blood out of my mind. But life goes on and Eric and I weren't what you would call close."

Kowalski pounced. "But you knew him well enough to hate him, didn't you? Here, look at this painting. I'm sure you remember it—and why you slashed it like that."

"Of course I do. It was that climatic scene two weeks ago where Kristen confronted Raven in her apartment for not only stealing her husband, but doing it unfairly. We used a combination of trick photography and a double.

During the fight, Kristen tore this portrait of Brock off the wall and ripped into it with a knife. It's a very Freudian scene, I was told, something to do with the Electra complex."

Kowalski sat down hard. "Are you seriously telling me that this painting was just a prop and —"

The door opened behind him. "Lieutenant?"

He turned around. "Can't you see I'm busy, Rico?"

"Sure, Lieutenant, but Jackson told me where you were and I thought you'd like to talk to this kid." He pushed in front of him a short slim young man with messy hair and peach fuzz above his lip.

Gillian jumped to her well-shod feet. "Billy! What are you doing here?"

"Guess I kind of screwed up, Ms. Burke," he mumbled.

She turned to the policemen. "Billy is a page for the studio. He has a terrible crush on me. I finally had to ask him to stop hanging around me because he was neglecting his job on another floor. I haven't seen him since. But what's he done that's so awful, Sergeant?"

"William Goebbels, age nineteen," Carlotta said for Kowalski's benefit. "I found him skulking around the sets."

"Oh, all right, you've got me," the page said miserably. "I might as well just confess and get it over with."

Kowalski and Carlotta looked at each other. What was this—Christmas?

"Please be our guest," Kowalski said. "You have the right to remain silent. Anything you say or do..." He recited the complete Miranda warning. No way was he going to risk the confession being thrown out on a procedural issue!

"Aw, come on," Billy said at the end, a stunned look on his face. "I know I was stupid, but it wasn't *that* big a deal.'"

"Killing a man wasn't a big deal?" Carlotta said.

"Killing?" His voice went up an octave. "What are you talking about, man? I stole the tape of the show. I don't know anything about any killing."

I should have known this wasn't going to be that easy, Kowalski thought. "You're halfway there, kid. You might as well man up to the whole enchilada. If you stole the tape, what possible motive could you have other than to force the episode to be done over so you could kill Eric Lord?"

"Mr. Lord is dead?" Billy swallowed like a Warner Brothers cartoon character. "I didn't know that! When Ms. Burke told me to bug off, I got real mad. I wanted to do something to hurt her, to mess things up bad. That's why I stole the tape. I was just hanging around today to see what happened because this is the day the tape was supposed to be on the air."

"Oh, Billy!" Gillian Burke appealed to Kowalski. "I'm sure he's telling the truth, Lieutenant. That sounds just like him. What possible motive would he have for killing Eric?"

"Try jealousy."

"Well, if you mean romantic jealousy, he certainly had no reason to be jealous of Eric Lord on my account. And as for that painting —"

"Hey, I remember that painting," Carlotta said, noticing it for the first time. "That was when Kristen and Raven went at each other a few weeks back. Does that have something to do with the case, Lieutenant?"

Kowalski sighed deeply. "I guess not."

✗ ✗ ✗ ✗

"So this is out last interview?" Carlotta asked as they rode up the elevator of a building on Central Park West two hours later.

"That's right, Rico. And maybe our last hope."

"How come we're going to her apartment instead of talking to her at the studio?"

"Because this is where Sondra Wentworth works. Apparently she's almost eighty and has been head writer on the show forever. She only goes to the studio once a week or so."

"But she had to know before the taping of today's episode that Brock McKenna was going to be killed off. If she wanted to use the TV shooting to kill Eric Lord, she could have done it then."

"Not if her motive is something that just popped up." That didn't seem likely even to Kowalski, but neither was it impossible.

He rang the doorbell, producing a pleasant chime. The last note barely faded away when the door opened on a statuesque woman with beautiful silver hair, shoulder length and wavy. She was elegantly dressed in a gray turtle neck sweater and a long black skirt. The pearls around her neck didn't look like the costume stuff Kowalski's mother had worn.

"You must be the police," she said. "How exciting!"

That was a new one. "I'm Lieutenant Kowalski. We talked on the phone. This is Sergeant Carlotta."

"I'm a big fan of 'Tomorrow is Another Day'," Carlotta gushed.

She looked him over. "Handsome and easily entertained. What a wonderful combination. I approve. I don't know how I can help the police, but please come in."

Sondra Wentworth's apartment, from the expensive furniture to the (probably genuine) Andy Warhol on the wall, was worlds removed from the soap opera family room where Kowalski spent much of his day. She'd done very well for herself, either at earning money or at marrying it.

"I can't get over the feeling that I am in some way responsible for Eric's death," the writer said, firing up a cigarette with a crystal lighter. In another era, Kowalski thought, she would have been smoking through a long black cigarette holder like Jessica Rabbit. "After all, I wrote the storyline that someone took advantage of to kill him. I am quite distraught."

"You shouldn't be," Kowalski said. "It's not your fault—unless, of course, you slipped the fatal bullet into the prop gun. You didn't, did you? Just for the record."

"Don't be absurd. Of course not."

"What were your relations with the victim?"

"I don't know that you could say we really had any. In my experience, Mr. Lord was not a friendly man."

"I've heard that he was *very* friendly with the ladies."

"With the *young* ladies. I don't qualify. Hell, I created 'Tomorrow is Another Day' before half the actors on it now were born."

"You must know everything about the show," Carlotta said. "So level with us, what happens next?"

His interest seemed more than professional to Kowalski.

Sondra Wentworth blew a meditative stream of smoke. "We don't write as far ahead as some soaps, Sergeant. The folks at General Brands, our chief sponsor, want us to be quick to respond to social media and the hot topics of the day. The next four weeks are written, and two of them are taped, but even I don't know whether Brock McKenna is going to live or die after that. I can tell you this, though: In the story meetings, I'm going to argue that Brock should recover. I'm sorry if this is in poor taste, but Brock returning to the show after the hubbub over Eric's murder would cause a sensation. I can see a major blowout on the cover of *Soap Opera Secrets*."

Kowalski spoke gently, as if he were talking to a crazy woman. He thought maybe he was. "How can that happen? Eric Lord is dead, Ms. Wentworth."

"Dead, yes, but replaceable. We could always bring back Art Morgan."

"What do you mean?"

"Art originated the part years ago."

"I didn't know that!" Carlotta exclaimed.

"Then he left to play that disreputable defense attorney on 'The Sands of Time' after a salary dispute. But his character was written out of that show early this year, so Art's available again. That happens all the time on soaps—actors leaving for another show, sometimes coming back later. From what I hear, Art probably would be willing to take Larry's terms now."

Kowalski smelled red meat. "So if Eric Lord was out of the picture, there was a fair chance that Morgan could get his old job back—and at a time when he needed one. All he had to do was bump off a guy who'd made passes at his wife. Come on, Rico, we've got to have another chat with that guy. You have the address of his apartment, don't you?"

✗ ✗ ✗ ✗

At about the same time, Arthur Morgan was having a difference of opinion with Mindy Stark as they left the studio in a taxi.

"I told you I'm okay, Art. I'm a big girl."

Morgan sulked, feeling that his protective instincts had been rebuffed. "I still don't think you should do 'The Yolanda Clark Show' right now. You look shook up to me. I know it's a good gig and your agent has been angling for it for months, but you sure as hell don't need the publicity at this point. You'll get more of that than you want in the next few days."

"But if I back out, it will look like I have something to hide. Relax. Fix us something nice for dinner."

"I'll do better than that. I'll make us a reservation at Twenty-One. Say about seven?"

"Fine. See you there."

They kissed, not as long as Morgan would have liked.

A few minutes later, the cab left Morgan off at the apartment building on West 10th Street where he and Mindy lived. He passed the doorman, Sam, with a conventional comment about the fineness of the weather and proceeded inside. Just as the elevator doors were closing, an elderly woman squeezed in. Morgan had a nagging feeling that he knew her from somewhere as he pushed the button for the eighteenth floor. *Wasn't she —?*

"Excuse me. I'm Maggie Dunbar. And you're Bart Tolliver, aren't you?"

Dunbar—the editor of Soap Opera Secrets*! Best to humor her.*

"Yeah, sure, I'm Bart Tolliver."

"But you're Brock McKenna, too. You can't fool me, you nasty man. I killed you once, you know."

"The hell you say!" Morgan unconsciously backed away in the small confines of the elevator car.

"Myrna acted like *she* was going to kill you, but she really just wanted to scare you. Why else would she put blanks in the gun? But then somehow it all happened over again and I was clever—I replaced the blanks with real bullets and you died. Only now you're back alive and I have to kill you again so Derek can have Myrna back and that nice young Luke Savage will be with Fane." She reached into her shoulder bag and pulled out a gun. Morgan could feel his heart pounding in his chest. The way this nutball was talking, there was no telling what she might do.

He put up his hands slowly, no sudden moves to agitate her. Even a lunatic couldn't miss a shot at this distance. "Easy, Maggie."

She pointed the gun squarely at his chest. "And if Raven doesn't leave town so Quint and Kristen can get back together, well, I'll just have to kill her, too."

Morgan swallowed, his throat dry as a desert, as he tried to remember all the times he'd played a scene like this with cameras rolling. "Be very careful, Maggie." He made his voice soothing, reassuring. "You don't really want to shoot. You want to put the gun back in your bag before it goes off and hurts one of us."

The magazine editor's expression was grim, although her misapplied lipstick made it look like she was smiling. "Oh, one of us is going to be hurt, all right, Mr. McKenna-Tolliver—and it's going to be you!"

At that moment, just as Morgan braced to make a desperate leap at the armed woman, the elevator stopped with a little jolt. The doors opened on the eighteenth floor to reveal the two policemen who had been at the studio earlier. The shocked look on their faces must have mirrored Morgan's. Maggie Dunbar, equally surprised, turned her gun toward the lawmen. The cops crouched as they pulled their weapons, she fired over their heads and Morgan shoved her from behind (just as he had done in a minor role on "Law and Order")—all within seconds. Dunbar fell into the hallway, where the sergeant pinned her with his foot and the lieutenant grabbed her gun.

"You're making a big mistake," she called. "You don't understand."

"I sure don't," Kowalski said with a sigh.

✗　✗　✗　✗

"Half the people we talked to acted like the storyline of 'Tomorrow is Another Day' was real—including you," Kowalski told Carlotta hours later at McGuire's Bar & Grill. "But it never entered my head that the killer could be somebody so deluded and so obsessed that she'd kill an actor for the bad things the character did on the show."

His sergeant shuddered theatrically. "She might have killed every villain on daytime TV if we hadn't been at Morgan's apartment." He took a long pull on his Smithwick's.

"Pure luck," Kowalski said, "and I made that clear in my report."

Carlotta's chin fell.

"So, you were expecting maybe a prominent mention leading to a promotion? Cheer up, Rico, I got you something better than that."

"A raise?"

"Even better. I got you a bit part in a future episode of 'Tomorrow is Another Day.' You get to help Detective Hopper investigate Brock McKenna's shooting. Good luck with the case." Kowalski drained his bourbon.

"Thanks, Lieutenant. But who needs luck? Didn't I say when we first met Maggie Dunbar that she looked awfully cheerful about Lord's murder? Maybe you should have paid more attention to me."

✗

THE MYSTERY OF THE PAUL HENRY

Michael Penncavage

SPRING 1889

"**H**ow are sales faring for the month, Linus?" asked Edmund as he walked over to an open window to light his cigarette, mindful of his partner's intolerance for the fumes.

About to settle down with his afternoon, Linus reluctantly placed his cup back onto the saucer and opened the ledger book.

"Slightly over last month," Linus replied. The gentlemen from Bangladesh who needed passage of his tigers back to India put us over the top."

Edmund exhaled a plume of smoke. "Excellent. If we keep at this rate we most certainly will be able to close up shop during July." He looked around the room with disdain. "New York is absolutely unbearable during the summer."

Linus closed the ledger and placed it on the shelf behind his desk. "And where do you plan on traveling?"

"Canada. Montreal to be specific. The cooler climate will keep my nerves in check…"

Knuckles rapped against the office door. Before they could respond a barrel-chested man who came hurrying in, wide-eyed and pale faced. He removed his cap and clenched in it his hands.

"Mr. Edmund Jessop? Mr. Linus Gordon?" He asked looking at them expectantly.

Edmund nodded. "We are they," he asked, looking over the man. "Which vessel did you sail in from, Captain?"

The man looked at Edmund bewildered as he ran his hand throw his thick salt and pepper hair. "How did you know that, sir?"

"Callused, cracked hands such as yours do not come from working indoors." He gestured to an empty chair. "Please have a seat."

He was visibly distressed as he continued to mash his hat in his hands. "My name is Frank Saverfeld. Captain of the *Paul Henry*."

"Would you care for a cup of tea, Captain?" asked Linus.

"No thank you. I am fine."

Edmund sat down next to the man. "You seem agitated, sir. Has availability opened up on your vessel that you need assistance in finding another client?"

"No. Quite the contrary." He paused for a moment as he looked at the two men. "Is it true that both of you served in the British Merchant Navy?"

Linus nodded. "Yes. I was a Steward aboard the *Sea Mist* while Edmund served as Boatswain."

Captain Saverfeld nodded. "Good. I'm glad I was not misinformed. I've heard of how you solved the Bonnington Mystery aboard the *Sea Mist* while you served under it."

Edmund cordially smiled. "That was a long time ago, Captain, and I'm afraid that the story has somewhat warped over the years. I'm certain the truth is not nearly as sensational as the version you've most likely heard."

The Captain shook his head. "That maybe so. But let me ask, if you not for your intellects, would more lives have been lost on the ship?"

Linus waved it dismissingly. "We merely added the facts, my good man. Nothing more."

Saverfeld practically bounced off his seat with excitement. "And that is precisely why I need your help! I am at my wits end, gentlemen. My wits end."

"Have you contacted the police?" asked Linus.

"I've spoken to the authorities but…"

"Why don't you share with us the details of your story, Captain Saverfeld?" said Edmund.

"It was during my last voyage. I had a hull brimming with sugar cane bound from South America. About three days into the journey one of my men, Rogers, was found in the galley dead."

"What time of day was he found?" asked Edmund.

"Dawn. Our Steward found him when he arrived to prepare the morning chow. He found Rogers slumped over a table."

"Any evidence as to how he was killed?"

"None what so ever. No knife wounds or bludgeoning could be located on his body. But what troubled me most was his death mask."

"Please explain," said Edmund.

"It was his eyes, Mr. Jessop. Wide and white as I ever did see a pair. And his mouth was open and contorted as if he had experienced such agony I can not even fathom."

"Sounds like a heart seizure," said Linus.

Saverfeld shook his head. "The man was in good shape. Strong like an ox. Good with his fists. Once we had an unruly sailor on our hands midway through a voyage. It looked like we were going to have to the lock the bloke up for the remainder of the trip. But all it took was two blows from Rogers's fists and the man became as quiet as a church mouse until we made landfall."

"Perhaps he had too much to drink? All it takes is one awkward swell to loose your footing."

"Impossible. I keep the grog under lock and key. While we are underway it is strictly rationed out based on how well the Mates keep the ship maintained.

"Did this man, Rogers, have any enemies on board?"

"Not at all. He treated the men under his command with respect. It was sad day indeed when we slid his body off to Davy Jones."

Linus crossed his legs. "Don't take this the wrong way, Captain, but I fail to see what help we can bring to you with this. It all sounds like a rather routine, though horribly unfortunate event. We are sailors, not inspectors."

"Absolutely, sir. But there's more to the tale," said the Captain. "Four nights later a scream bellowed near the bow. My Second Mate, who was near the stern, keeping an eye on matters, raced towards the noise, fearful that one of the men had taken a spill overboard."

"What did he find?" asked Linus.

"Simon Bettany, one of Hands, was lying on his side, stiff as a board. My Second instructed one of the sailors to go and fetch me while he kept watch over the body. I arrived minutes later from my cabin, and had the entire area lanterned up so we could properly examine the body."

"Bettany was in the same condition as Rogers. No visible signs of injury," replied the Captain. "But the look on his face..." He paused for a moment as if ashamed to continue. "It was as if the man had been scared to death."

Edmund and Linus said nothing as they listened intently.

"We were still some distance away from port. The day after Bettany died a slack wind fell upon the ship just as we entered the Southern Tropics. It was then that things went from bad to worse."

"What do you mean?" asked Linus.

"A rumor broke out amongst the crew that Bettany and Rogers had been befallen by a ghost."

Linus placed his tea cup down. "A ghost?"

The Captain shook his head. "I don't know how it started, but between the queer way in which they died as well as the idle time the crew found themselves with due to the slack wind, the rumor festered. With each passing night the Hands began to share stories about seeing shadows in the darkened corners and hearing noises that they were certain wasn't creaking boat timber. I tried my best to keep the hands busy with cleaning and scrubbing. I even cut off the grog to one cup per day. But the heat and the poor winds began to win over the crews' nerves. Each evening brought more stories and more tension, so much so that I feared there might be a mutiny on my hands. Fortunately, we passed out of the doldrums. An ease passed over the crew. I thought we'd been through the worst of it."

"But another murder occurred," continued Edmund.

"Yes. The night after we came out of the doldrums. Peter Mulberry, one of the deckhands was found dead in his bunk."

"The same causes?"

Saverfeld nodded. "The cabins were scorching so only a few hands ventured down below to sleep. Mulberry was alone in his cabin when he died. But there was one disturbing difference about his death. The door was closed and bolted from the inside."

"That seems odd that he would have locked the door," commented Linus. "Considering that he shared the room with other sailors."

"Nerves were still on edge. There were those who believed a killer was on board. Mulberry likely locked the door as a precaution to make sure he wasn't snuck up on while he napped."

Edmund shook his head. "A testament to your leadership, Captain, that you were able to keep the crew together for the remainder of the voyage."

"It wasn't easy, Mr. Jessop. After Mulberry died I had to keep a good amount of the crew under lock and key. It was only due to the few Hands who had maintained a clear head and the fortunate weather that I was able to sail the *Paul Henry* safely into port."

Edmund put out his cigarette. "A most unsettling story. You mentioned after you docked that you had gone to the authorities to discuss the matter?"

The Captain shook his cap in frustration. "Yes. I spoke to the Captain of the local police force. After much persuasion on my part, he took a couple of his men, did a cursory review of my ship, and deemed nothing wrong."

"Nothing wrong!" echoed Linus incredulously.

"All of the bodies had been delivered to the ocean. And the scenes of the deaths, with the exception of Mulberry's, had been wiped clean by the wind and the sea. And even though I allowed no one entry to Mulberry's room, the police were able to find nothing out of the ordinary."

"Not even the slightest clue?" asked Linus.

Saverfeld shook his head.

Edmund rubbed his chin thoughtfully. "A set of most peculiar events, Captain. I am sorry the police did get you the satisfaction that you sought."

"I feel part of the reason was that the deaths did not occur on native soil. They aren't like us, gentlemen. They're land lovers. I'm afraid they might have overlooked something important. That is why I came to seek your help, Mr. Jessop.

"You wish us to visit the *Paul Henry* and have a look around, first hand?" asked Linus.

"In a manner of speaking."

"You wish us to *voyage* with you," corrected Edmund.

"Why, yes," stammered Saverfeld. "In one week's time the *Paul Henry* is scheduled to take a shipment of tea to London en-route from the Orient."

"Quite a pricey payload," remarked Edmund. "A shipload of tea and a jittery crew make for a volatile combination."

"Exactly. And that is what has me so worried." Saverfeld wiped his brow. "I am prepared to be quite generous in my offer of convincing you to join me on the journey."

"A trip to London is quite an undertaking, Captain," said Linus.

"Yes. But something nefarious is transpiring on my ship, gentlemen. Something evil and something I can't explain. I been on the sea all of my life and seen all manner of dastardly business. But nothing I have experienced has equaled the horror and dread that I felt during this past voyage. All I am certain of is that I need someone with your skills to help me deal with it if this happens again."

"When do you depart?" asked Edmund.

"This Sunday morning. At dawn."

"If you would please let my partner and I discuss your proposal. We will send a letter regarding our decision by midweek."

"But you haven't heard my offer."

"And a most generous one it certainly will be," said Edmund. "One last question, Captain. Does anyone know of your trip to see us?"

"No one, sir."

"Very good. I would appreciate it if you kept it that way."

Captain Saverfeld nodded as he rose from his chair. "I will leave you then to your deliberations, then." With that the burly man put his wrinkled cap back on, shook hands with Edmund and Linus, and bid them good-day.

✗ ✗ ✗ ✗

The wooden planks protested loudly as Edmund and Linus walked out onto the pier. The smells were heavy there. Salt and brine mostly, but other scents, such as flats of salted meats and barrels of apples filled the air as they were loaded on the *Paul Henry*.

Edmund approached a man at the base of the gangplank. He was short and stocky, with a balding head and reddish nose. The First Mate. He glanced up at Edmund and Linus before burying his face back in the clipboard. "Name?" he grumbled.

Edmund scratched his newly grown stubble of a beard. "Edmund Sullivan," he answered, choosing to go with his mother's maiden name.

The First looked at Linus with the same scowl. "Linus Grovestead."

"Steward and Deckhand is what I've got you both down for. I'm Keller. You two aware of the problems this boat had on its trip into port?"

"I've heard some rumors," replied Linus.

"That sort of thing gonna bother you?" asked the Mate. "They're saying the boat is haunted."

"Only thing gonna bother us is not getting paid," said Linus.

"Be warned that aboard the *Paul Henry* any bad-behavior by the crew is rewarded by fifteen lashes and a trip to the brig."

"If I didn't know any better," said Edmund. "I would think you didn't want us to come aboard."

Keller thumbed over his shoulder. "Your bunks are down below."

✗ ✗ ✗ ✗

The Second Mate, Henry Tilleray was in complete contrast to Keller. The man practically walked with a spring in his step as he briefly toured them through the ships' quarters.

"Happy to be back on the water?" asked Edmund.

"I've never been much of a land lover," replied Tilleray. "Stable ground is only meant for people to be buried in. And for me, not even that," he sighed. "Been on the sea my entire life."

"More than just the trade routes?" inquired Edmund.

He nodded. "Assisted in some exploring jaunts with a few fortune seekers," answered the Second. "Traveled all over. Like Sinbad traveling the Seven Seas."

Linus noticed the sparcity of the crew's quarters. "Got a skeleton crew for this trip?"

"That'd be putting it mildly. "The bare minimum. Any of the Hands get injured during this trip and we might be in a pickle."

"I heard about the troubles with the last voyage," said Edmund.

"Either of you blokes superstitious?"

Neither answered.

"That's good," commented Tilleray. "Lots of jittery Mates on board. Last thing the Captain needs is two more."

"A lot of the crew fled once you made port?"

"A good number. Except for a few hardy souls, and a few, like yourselves, who don't seem to mind the notion of a ship being haunted. At least for now." He stopped at one of the cabins. It was a tight affair, with room for four bunks and eight men. "Here you are. All to yourself. I suppose this is one good thing of traveling with a light crew." He turned to Edmund. "Stow your belongings and report to the Galley." And then to Linus, he said. "Report to the deck in five minutes." He left.

They began settling in. "Just like old times, eh?" commented Linus as he took a deep breath in, lost in thought for a moment. "Did you brush up on your culinary talents and review your cookbooks?"

"Somewhat. Though as we both know, I won't be preparing quite the same cuisine as they served on the *Sea Mist*." They shared a chuckle before he added. "But remember to be alert, my friend. Something is terribly amiss on this ship. And we best be careful not to let it get us before we uncover it."

✗ ✗ ✗ ✗

No sooner had Linus left then a boy appeared in the doorway. He had sandy blonde hair and a face full of sun freckles. "You the new Steward?" he asked with pronunciation that made Edmund cringe. "I'm Yancy. Assistant Steward. Captain asked me to come and show you the galley and where we store the goods."

"Very well," answered Edmund. "You've been serving under Captain Saverfeld for a long time?"

"Almost two years. Cap'n treats me and the other Mates well, so I've decided to hang around a bit more."

"And this business that has been going on hasn't made you want to reconsider?"

"The boy crossed his arms defiantly. "It'll take more than a few spookes to scare me off. Unlike the previous Steward who went running for the hills as soon as we docked."

The boy reminded him of himself at that age. "What do you think the crew would like to eat on their first night out?"

Yancy stared at him, thrown off by the question. If Edmund was going to acquire some allies on the ship, who better to start with than someone who could go anywhere on the boat without drawing any attention?

"I think the Hands would enjoy some salted pork. To help calm their nerves about them spooks."

They began walking towards the galley. "I almost forgot," said Yancy as he dug into his pocket and removed an envelope. "Captain told me to give this to you. Didn't tell me what it was for."

There was a slight weight to the envelope. "Thank you, Yancy. I will meet you in the Galley in a short while."

The boy went heading off and Edmund unsealed the envelope. Inside was a brass key and a slip of paper with a number scribbled on it.

Mulberry's room.

✗ ✗ ✗ ✗

The Hand's room was identical to his own. Mulberry's bunk still had his possessions tucked away in it.

Edmund sifted through the man's belongings but found little of interest, remembering that if there had been something deemed important, or more specifically, *valuable*, the police would have taken it.

There was a single open porthole in the room, which was allowing for a fair amount of daylight to filter in. Mulberry's bunk was closest to it, which meant that even in this meager little room, Mulberrry had seniority.

He walked over to the porthole, which was six inches across, and looked out. The Hands were just about to cast off.

Edmund swung the porthole latch closed but it didn't stay shut. The clasp which kept it shut was broken. A slight tug on the latch made the porthole reopen.

The bunk was hard and uncomfortable. He looked up at the window. Edmund listened as the waves lapped against the hull. They sounded different than just a moment ago and Edmund knew it meant only one thing.

They were underway.

✗ ✗ ✗ ✗

Later that evening Linus found Edmund near the bow of the ship, smoking.

"Dinner was impeccable," he said, grinning.

"You're a poor liar, my friend. There is only so much you can do with a meal where the main ingredient is salt."

Linus began to chuckle. "Ah, the old days. Makes you wish for them again."

"I miss them as much as I do scurvy. When we left the *Sea Mist* I swore I would never let the food on these boats touch my lips." Edmund sighed as he looked out over the calm waters. A favorable starboard wind had been with them since they had left port and already New York had disappeared over the horizon. "How are the Hands faring?"

"Not bad. But there is an underlying uneasiness."

"Have any rumors spread? Any of the crew imagining seeing things?"

Linus chuckled. "Always the cynic, eh, Edmund?"

"Pragmatist, my friend. Simply a pragmatist. Show me a man who can spin these tales without a belly full of grog and that man will command my utmost attention."

"Good evening, gentlemen," boomed a familiar voice. Captain Saverfeld appeared from the starboard, his massive frame filling up the staircase as he descended down the stairs to the Bow Deck. "Excellent meal," he commended, lighting up his pipe. At the very least, money well spent there."

"Thank you, Captain."

Saverfeld looked out over the water. "Favorable conditions tonight. Excellent way to begin our voyage." He exhaled a plume of smoke. "I realize we are just underway, but you have any thoughts as to what might be going on?"

Edmund puffed on his cigarette. "It's still too early to share with you any firm thoughts. However, I would suggest you take every precaution necessary to ensure your safety. Supernatural or not, there is a threat onboard this ship."

Saverfeld was taken aback. "But the only people left on the *Paul Henry* are my most trusted Hands…"

A bell began to ring from the stern of the ship. "Oh, no. This can not be."

"Captain, what is wrong?" asked Linus.

"That bell. The crew has instructions to ring it there has been a sighting."

The men sprinted to the rear of the vessel, until they came across a small group of Hands.

"Stand aside, lads. Stand aside," barked Saverfeld as he plowed through the sailors.

The men all sported a worried expression. One of them, Stevenson, spoke up. "I saw it, Captain."

"Saw *what*, man?"

"I was coming round the port side when I saw this large shadow scurry across right in front of me. I tried chasing it but it disappeared around the square rig and then vanished from sight."

"You sure your eyes aren't playing tricks on ya, Stevenson? Moon's particularly full tonight. Could have been the topsail casting shadows over the deck."

"No, Captain. I know when I'm seeing shadows and when I..."

Saverfeld had heard enough. "*And* when you haven't seen anything at all, which is what happened here." He glared at the rest of the hands. "Now, either you all get down below and get some shut-eye or we can all get an early start on scrubbing the decks!"

Edmund and Linus walked over to where Stevenson had seen the shadow. It was the port side. Besides a few open portholes there were no places for someone to hide.

Keller walked up to them. "You two gone deaf? Back below!"

Edmund turned to the First. "Where do those portholes lead to?"

Keller seemed shocked to have been spoken back to. "Why do you want to know?"

"If you would just humor me, Mr. Keller."

"Officer's quarters, such as my own, if you are so interested."

Edmund smiled and began walking towards the crew's entrance. "Sullivan!" barked Keller. "All of these questions." He pointed a fat finger at Edmund. "I'll be watching you."

✗ ✗ ✗ ✗

Three days passed without incident. It was evening and Edmund was cleaning up around his small kitchen when he heard a gasp quickly followed by a shriek come from the galley. Edmund grabbed the cast iron pan he had been cleaning and came rushing into the room.

Yancy was lying on the floor. His eyes were wide open and he was gasping for breath as if some unseen presence was suffocating the boy.

Edmund rushed over and knelt down next to him. Yancy looked at him, grasping his shirt, trying to speak what was wrong, but no words came out.

He opened the boy's mouth, trying to see if he was choking when he noticed the color of his tongue. It was black.

Yancy gasped again, shuttered a few times, and fell limp in Edmund's arms.

✗ ✗ ✗ ✗

With Yancy's death, the crew was quickly worked up into a nervous fervor. At first light Saverfeld gathered all Hands on deck for a talking to.

He placed his hands behind his back and paused for a moment before speaking. "I realize the death of our young Steward has caught everyone by surprise. Let me assure you that his death will be fully investigated..."

"You gonna try and arrest the devil, Cap'n?" yelled one of the hands from the crowd.

"They'll be no back-talking to the Captain!" shouted Keller. "Not until anyone feels like spending a few days in the brig."

This settled the mates down somewhat, except for one who shouted. "Investigated by who, Captain? By the time we reach port all the clues will be goners."

"This time things are different, lads. This time I've got an investigator on board." He turned to Edmund. Linus, meanwhile had moved to the rear of the crowd, away from his partner.

"Cap'n gone mad," someone yelled. "That's the cook."

"I've hired Edmund Jessop back in New York to help me figure out what is going on board of our ship."

"Only thing going on, Cap, is that the whole bloody vessel is haunted…" The Hand was cut off by Tilleray who spotted the instigator and clubbed the man from behind, sending him to the ground.

Saverfeld continued. "Mr. Jessop believes he has almost solved what has been transpiring aboard our ship. He has told me that he needs just a little more time, at which point he will inform me of his learnings."

Edmund took a step closer to the Captain and spoke. "I realize all of you are uneasy at the present time. Let me *assure* all of you that the truth behind these murders will be brought to light in short order."

"Gonna put the ghosty in shackles, are you?" joked one of the Hands, which started a short burst of laughter from the rest of the crowd.

"All in good time, my man. All in good time."

Saying that, the First stepped up next to Edmund and began barking orders. At once the crowd dispersed.

✗ ✗ ✗ ✗

Later that night, Edmund, Linus, and Saverfeld were in the Captain's quarters, sitting around the Chart Table. Maps, compasses, sextants, and other nautical apparatus covered the surface as well as three glasses of brandy.

Concern blanketed Saverfeld's face. "I don't like this, Mr. Jessop. I don't like it one bit."

"Not to worry, Captain. You played your part masterfully."

Saverfeld gripped his drink and swallowed what remained in the glass. "The only thing I did was shine a light on you, sir. Now, every move you make you will be watched."

"I sincerely hope so, Captain! It would have been most unfortunate if you had given your speech and our ghost was not in attendance." Edmund noticed Saverfeld's pistol holstered to his belt. "Continue to have your weapon nearby, Captain. Oiled and loaded please. With any luck we will have an end to this sordid business before the sun rises."

✗ ✗ ✗ ✗

Linus and Edmund sat in opposite bunks. The porthole was open and slight breeze trickled into the room. Linus wiped his brow. "The one thing I definitely do not miss, Edmund, is the stifling heat of these ships."

"Perhaps tomorrow we will able to sleep beneath the stars."

"Had you told me a month ago that we would be setting sail for London in an attempt to solve some murders, I would have thought you a bit daft."

"As would have I," replied Edmund as he listened to the sounds outside. Water sloshed against the hull. They were making good time. Voices from some of the Hands on deck could be heard as well. Saverfeld had placed additional men on guard.

Edmund glanced at his pocket watch. "It's late." He removed "I don't think I will be sleeping for a while if you want to rest, Linus."

Linus gestured to the cabin door that had a wooden barrel in front of it. "No need to be concerned for our safety. If anyone is going to gain entry it's only going to be with a battering ram!"

"Ghosts don't need to worry about such trivial obstacles," Edmund said coyly.

Linus eyed his friend up for a moment. "You've figured it all out, haven't you? Well spill it, my man. Spill it."

"No need to put the cart in front of the horse. Not when I have a few questions that I still can't place. Perhaps if our ghost comes to visit they will provide some answers."

Linus placed his pistol beside him. "You'd best ask your questions quickly. Hot lead is going to be my answer if anyone tries breaking in!"

Edmund removed a stiletto from its sheath and didn't reply.

Linus dimmed the lantern so it emitted only the faintest of flickers. Outside, the crashing of waves continued to be heard until it lulled him off to sleep.

✗ ✗ ✗ ✗

Linus awoke to Edmund's cry of alarm. "Ah-hah! Back swine! Back!" Linus grabbed his revolver and bolted up from the cot. By the time he had managed to collect his bearings and turn up the lantern, Edmund was standing by the porthole, breathing hard, the dagger in his hand. Blood dripped from the blade.

"The door, Linus! There's not a moment to loose!"

"Our ghost bleeds?" cried Linus as he slid the barrel away. Edmund flung the door open to reveal a small stampede of men, Saverfeld included, rushing towards their room.

"Mr. Jessop!" cried Saverfeld as his eyes fell upon the bloodied dagger. "Are you all right? Are you injured?"

"Captain. You have your weapon?"

Saverfeld raised up a pistol.

"Excellent. Follow me. To the deck."

"What is wrong?"

"No time to explain, Captain!" Edmund yelled, rushing off. "Time is of the essence."

The score of men quickly rushed outside until they reached the side of the ship that had the porthole that lead into Edmund's room. "A lantern!" One of the Hands passed it to him. He crouched down at the surrounding deck face to the floor until he cried out. "Spots!" he said, pointing. "Our ghost's bloody trail. Follow it and we find our culprit."

This lead to gasps from several of the men. Saverfeld held up his pistol. "Weapons ready, men." This seemed to force a backbone into the crew as Edmund, lantern in hand, began to follow the trail of blood like a hound in pursuit of the fox.

They raced across the ship until the blood led then back below deck.

One of the Hands gasped. "We're heading straight into the Officer's Quarters." Through a corridor they raced until they came to a small pool of blood collected in front of one of the rooms.

"This can't be," gasped Saverfeld. "This is my Second's room."

"Mr. Tilleray," barked Edmund. "The rouse is over. I'd advise you to come out now if you want your Captain to show mercy."

There was no response from inside the cabin.

Saverfeld nodded to the burliest man in the crew. "Take it down," he ordered. The Mate shouldered up and brought the door down with two hard strikes. No sooner had he breached the room then he was met with a muzzle flash.

Tilleray's shot was quickly met by Saverfeld's gun. As the smoke cleared Tilleray was lying face down on the floor.

Edmund walked into the room, dagger drawn. Saverfeld charged into the room but was held back by Edmund. "Careful, Captain. The blood trail was not left by Mr. Tilleray."

His gun spent, Saverfeld unsheathed his cutlass.

"There! In the corner!" exclaimed Linus, pointing. "Someone shine a lantern!"

One of the crew did so and the shadowed figure became illuminated.

"It's some sort of monkey."

The group cautiously approached. The animal was no larger than a foot in size. It was huddled in the corner, and just like Tilleray, unmoving.

"The creature returned back to its master, where it finally succumbed to its wounds."

Saverfeld sheathed his sword. "Now hold on a moment, Mr. Jessop. Are you telling me this little bugger is responsible for murdering my crew?"

"Captain, I would suggest that we have the rest of this conversation in private."

The Boatswain cleared out the room.

"No one within thirty feet of this door!" instructed Saverfeld.

"The motive was clear," began Edmund. "To obtain your cargo and resell it to the highest bidder."

"How long did you know it was Tilleray?"

"Actually, I didn't. At first I thought your First Mate, Mr. Keller, might have been behind the plot."

"And you never thought it was some sort of ghost?"

"I believed that someone was trying their best to make it *seem* like a ghost. The one piece of the puzzle that was baffling me was Mulberry's death and how it had been accomplished. They lead me to reason that something more nefarious was occurring than I had originally suspected."

"How were they killed?" asked the Captain. "The bodies were thoroughly examined and no wounds were found."

Linus spoke up. "That was solved when the boy, Yancy was killed. For the first time I was able to examine the bodies and noticed the strange color of his tongue. It meant only one thing. He was poisoned."

"Poisoned? How?"

During the conversation Edmund had been slowly walking around the room, searching. "By poisoned dart." He picked up a small bamboo pipe, no larger than a flute. "Dispensed by this. Tilleray would have had access to the weapon as well as the poison during his travels to Central Africa. I'm sure if we do a thorough search of the room we will come across the poison."

The Captain considered this. "What you say makes sense. But again I ask, how did poor Mulberry die? Tilleray did not have entry to his room."

"This is the part that I struggled with the most. The most insidious acts of a crime are always the most difficult to comprehend." Edmund gestured over to the primate. "This is where the poor creature in the corner comes into play." He walked over to the monkey and carefully turned it over using the flat edge of his dagger. There, still clutched in its hand, was a small spike. "This is how Mulberry died. Tilleray had trained the animal to sneak into the man's room through the porthole and give him a small poke with the poisoned spike. Death was quick but not painless. Linus and I would have suffered the same fate had we not been able to fend off the creature before it attacked."

"But what about the sightings that took place on the ship? Were they simply from this monkey running amuck?"

"Yes. Sometimes even the smallest of creatures can seem like the largest of monsters when the mind starts playing tricks on you." Edmund lowered his voice. "There is something else to consider. That some of the stories and rumors being told were nothing more than lies."

"Saverfeld turned red in the face. "Mr. Jessop, are you suggesting…"

"I am simply stating that if Tilleray had planned to commit mutiny there would have been no way he would have been able to go about it alone."

The Captain clasped his hands together. "A mutiny on my ship. And I have no idea who these men might be."

Linus walked up to him. "Would you care for some advice, Captain?"

"Tell away, sir."

"While it is true you do not know who precisely these men are, there is no reason to let the crew know this fact."

"What do you mean?"

Edmund spoke up. "What my partner is proposing is a bluff. That you found a list in Tilleray's cabin listing his co-conspirators."

"I have?"

"You have. And tomorrow morning you will gather the men and announce that you have found this list in Tilleray's cabin," said Edmund. "But you are a forgiving man. And in your effort to forget past sins, you will not bring retribution to those involved."

Displeasure covered Saverfeld's face.

"Take your lumps, Captain. It's either that or you start tossing crew members in the brig with hopes that you are imprisoning the correct people. I believe that Tilleray was the head of the snake. Now that the head has been severed, this potential mutiny will wither away." Edmund lit a fresh cigarette. "When you arrive in port you release your entire crew and hire anew for your journey back to the States. Of course, present company excluded. The heat and humidity of the New York summers are suddenly very appealing to me."

THE PROBLEM OF THE VANISHING BULLET

Lee Enderlin

"Oh, no, Mr Holmes. My dear fiancé is most guilty of shooting Mr Smythe. I saw it myself. I was standing no further from them than I am from you and Dr Watson right now."

While such a startling confession from our young and delicate visitor caused me to almost drop the cup of tea that Mrs Hudson had so thoughtfully provided, I must say that my friend, Mr Sherlock Holmes, barely raised an eyebrow.

It pained me that such an individual as our visitor should have witnessed so sordid a business. Miss Elizabeth Whitingham was, to the best of my estimation, perhaps 20 years old, perhaps a year or two less, but carried herself with great maturity. Her long, black hair was drawn back and she demurely drank her tea with tiny, white-gloved hands. I could imagine she suffered from no lack of suitors prior to her recent engagement to Mr James Hardwicke. A daughter of a family with some social connections, her betrothal was duly reported in the society columns, but it was of little interest to us until the arrest yesterday of Mr Hardwicke for the murder of Mr Smythe.

Having the honour of taking part in some of my friend's cases, I cannot say that I was surprised that Miss Whitingham should call upon Holmes. Those of privilege often did so at this stage of his career. All too often, however, they were merely attempting to buy Holmes' brilliance, hoping that he might find some clever, if false, way out of their troubles which were often of their own doing. Holmes routinely turned such cases down, saying, "When it comes to justice, Watson, I draw no distinction between rich man and poor man. The facts are the facts and they lead us where they will. The rich, however, frequently dangle their money in front of me to manipulate those facts. And," he added with a laugh, "always in their favour!"

This, I suspected, may have been the purpose of Miss Whitingham's visit that warm spring morning in 1903. According to the evening papers, Mr Hardwicke had been arrested for the murder of Mr Smythe following a rather heated argument. It seemed a pretty straightforward incident. Holmes, too, had evidently expected Miss Whitingham to beg him to play the role of clever manipulator for his first comment after Mrs Hudson's tea arrived was, "I suppose you'd like me to prove that Mr Hardwicke did not shoot Mr

Smythe, Miss Whitingam." I must admit I was a bit disappointed in his rather brusque manner toward our youthful guest.

Her surprising answer, of course, shocked us both, though Holmes' reaction was far more restrained than my own.

Holmes peered across the room, his interest I could hear in his voice if not see in his face, suddenly peaked. "What would you have me do then?"

Elizabeth Whittingham took a sip of her tea before answering. "There are many facts about the…incident…which were not reported, Mr Holmes. I would ask you to look into the affair and attempt to make some sense of them."

"And what, pray, would these facts be?"

"Mr Holmes, James, my fiancé, did indeed shoot Mr Smythe as I have stated. Of that, there is no doubt. However, and you must absolutely take my word for this, Mr Holmes, he shot him in self-defense."

"The police would not likely have arrested him so quickly if indeed it were a complicated case of self-defense," I noted. "In fact, they might not have arrested him at all. They seem quite assured that they have their man, so to speak. At least, that's the impression I got from the newspaper accounts."

"That's very true, Dr Watson. The police are quite adamant," our guest acknowledged. "However, I was there and I saw exactly what happened."

"Perhaps you can tell us, then, just what did take place, Miss Whitingham," Holmes encouraged her.

"There had been bad blood between James and Mr Smythe for quite some time, I'm afraid."

"Une affaire de coeur?" Holmes asked.

Our visitor blushed and lowered her eyes. "No, not at all, Mr Holmes, although that is a fair question. Indeed, I hardly knew Mr Smythe at all. It seems that their disagreements were strictly of a business nature. James hired Mr Smythe's company to do some renovating for him and he was quite unhappy with their work. I don't know all the particulars, but it appears that Mr Smythe's firm was chosen because of some great favour done in the past by one of Mr Smythe's antecedents for one of James' ancestors. Apparently, at least according to James, the current Mr Smythe did not adhere to the same scruples of his own ancestor."

"What was the nature of these disagreements?"

"Shoddy workmanship and, most of all, the use of cheap materials when far more expensive ones had not only been requested, but already paid for."

Holmes nodded silently in understanding. "And as to more recent events," he prompted.

Miss Whitingham continued. "Yesterday, Mr Smythe approached James as James was about to leave for some target shooting. I was there to discuss some matters concerning our upcoming nuptials when Mr Smythe burst into the room. I cannot say that he was roaring drunk, gentlemen, but clearly he had been drinking enough to cloud his judgment for he came in waving a revolver erratically. He accused James of sullying his name and business reputation, which was probably quite true for James was quite public in his criticism of Mr Smythe's work. Naturally, further words were exchanged, not very pleasant ones, I'm afraid, and James requested that Mr Smythe leave the premises."

"Where exactly were you?" Holmes asked.

"In James's study, Mr Holmes, at his home in Kensington. Instead of leaving, though, Mr Smythe continued to scream and threaten and eventually fired a shot at James who instinctively fired back. I'm sure James feared for my safety as well as his own. As drunk as he was, Mr Smythe's shot missed by a considerable margin while James was, if you'll excuse the expression, dead on the mark. He's a champion shot, you see. He's won many a competition."

"You were indoors?"

"That is correct, Mr Holmes."

Holmes sighed. "It would seem to be a simple matter of determining where Mr Smythe's bullet hit somewhere in the room, I should think. That would prove Mr Hardwicke's innocence or, at the very least, cloud up the issue of who shot first quite enough so that a jury would find reasonable doubt in favour of self-defense."

"If only it were that simple, Mr Holmes. You see, there is a minor complication."

"And what, pray, is that?"

"Mr Holmes, the bullet fired by Mr Smythe simply vanished into thin air."

Holmes' eyes widened. "Indeed?"

"Precisely. The bullet was fired at a blank wall, yet left no hole, no crack, nothing."

"The ceiling or another wall, perhaps?" I asked.

"The police were very thorough in their search, I'm afraid. They found no sign anywhere. And yet, I saw Mr Smythe fire his revolver clearly in the direction of the wall. I swear it."

I hated to deny the unfortunate thing her only hope of seeing the release of her fiancé, but even I could see the solution to this mystery. Holmes had little else to say and sat silently for a moment, seemingly contemplating the air between his upraised fingers.

"What sort of man was Mr Smythe when he was sober?"

"Gruff, I would say, but not violent."

"Had he ever confronted Mr Hardwicke before?"

"Several times. Always the same story. Words were exchanged, but nothing more. James accused Mr Smythe of cheating and threatened legal action. Mr Smythe vehemently denied the charges. Eventually, James had Mr Smythe's company completely stop the work. It remains unfinished still, most of it in the very room where this awful…thing…took place. But never before, however, was violence involved. Just angry words."

Holmes listened to her quietly. "I'll look into the matter, Miss Whitingham. You may hear from me as early as this afternoon."

Holmes' announcement surprised me. He was normally not one to waste time on the obvious. With that, Miss Whitingham thanked us and took her leave. We saw her out and after she left, I turned back to the room to see Holmes tamping down his tobacco.

"Well, I must say, Holmes, perhaps you are a bit more affected by the opposite sex than you admit."

"How so, Watson?"

"Why have you agreed to help Miss Whitingham? The solution to her problem is quite obvious. Could it be that you find it difficult to simply say no to a lovely young lady?"

"Watson, I am not so much a machine that I could not help but notice our visitor's obvious charms. But no, I agreed to help her only because I am curious."

"About what? Clearly Mr Smythe used a stage blank."

"A distinct possibility, Watson. However, as I mulled it over, one nagging question came to mind."

"What is that?"

"Why would a man, even one somewhat in his cups, fire a stage blank at another man whose pistol is obviously loaded? Mr Hardwicke's weapon would certainly not be loaded with stage blanks—he was a champion shooter heading off to practice.'

Again, I am embarrassed to admit that Holmes had seen something I had overlooked.

"I can think of only one reason," he continued. He paused as if the thought should be an apparent one. He knew I would ask.

"What, Holmes?"

"Suicide. However, giving up one's life to simply incriminate another seems a heavy price to pay. Why not simply shoot your rival outright?"

"We've run across it before as I'm sure you remember. At Thor Bridge."

"Precisely. What are the odds that we should see such demented and radical behavior again? Besides, the tragic Mrs Gibson was extremely cold and calculating not to mention a bit addled. Mr Smythe had been drinking and was acting in anger. Not the sort of condition for a cold, calculating deed. I may leave the opposite sex to your department, Watson, but I do understand the motivations of men. I believe Mr Smythe came to Mr Hardwicke with murder in his heart."

"You're saying, then, that my theory is wrong."

"Not at all, Watson. Just highly improbable. We do not have all of the facts and there are aspects of this case that have me most curious."

"But if Mr Smythe did not use stage blanks, then where is the bullet?"

Holmes stared a long time across the room. His patriotic "**V. R.**" in bullet marks stained our own wall. It hung in front of him like a dark, gigantic spider's web—his own empirical proof that bullets do indeed make notice-able marks in plaster.

"That is precisely what I am most curious about," he said simply.

Holmes sat stone still. I dared not interrupt his reverie. After a time, he stood and said, "Let's be off, Watson. There are places to go."

"Where to?"

"I think we'll stop for a chat with Mr Hardwicke first."

"Not to the scene first?"

"I think not. Lestrade's people have trampled the place beyond redemption by now. Besides, the Yard is more or less on our way to Kensington. Another hour's delay will change nothing. I should like to see if Mr Hardwicke's story corroborates that of his fiancée. Vanishing bullets simply do not exist any more than the incident at Thor Bridge proved that vanishing pistols do not exist. I should like to know if Mr Hardwicke 'saw' the vanishing bullet, as well."

The ride to Scotland Yard was a pleasant one despite our mission. The growing warmth of the day foretold of the coming of spring and the end of winter. I suspect all of this was lost on Holmes, who spoke not a word during our brief journey in the hansom.

At the Yard, we first had to make our way through the proper channels which, naturally, meant Lestrade. I could not but help reflect on the changes in attitude towards each other that had developed over the years. Holmes, while still despairing of Lestrade's analytical ability, had grown most re-spectful of his strength—that bulldog tenacity of his that once channeled, led to many a successful apprehension of a perpetrator. For his part, Lestrade had come to respect the unusual powers of my friend as well, helped in no small amount by the times that Holmes had let Lestrade take full credit for Holmes' own work. Their conversations, while often containing the very same words they had spoken to each other over the years, now carried more the flavour of friends bantering rather than the vicious invective of bitter rivals.

"I should like to have a word with James Hardwicke, Lestrade," Holmes said after the genuinely warm greetings were passed around.

"Ah, he's got you checking up on him now, has he?" Lestrade said as he led us to Hardwicke's cell. "Well, Holmes, I do believe this one's locked up tighter than a drum. Clear case of murder."

"Not self-defense?"

"Oh, he claims so, but there isn't a shred of evidence to back him up. If there's one thing I've learned from you over the years, Holmes, it's to be most through searching a crime setting. Hardwicke claims he shot second, but there's absolutely no evidence whatever of a shot from the victim."

"Have you checked both of their revolvers?"

"Indeed we have."

"And what have you found?"

"One shot fired from each pistol."

"Have you not just contradicted yourself?"

"Indeed not," Lestrade claimed proudly. "I said 'no evidence of a shot from the victim,' not 'no evidence of a shot from the victim's pistol.'"

"And you explain the hair-splitting difference how?"

"It's not at all splitting hairs, Holmes. In order to corroborate his claim of self-defense, Mr Hardwicke simply fired the victim's pistol himself. Out a window, likely, into the forest beyond."

Holmes raised an eyebrow. "Perhaps. Except for one thing."

"What is that, Holmes?"

"If a man is to claim self-defense, why not fire the bullet somewhere that it is easily found?"

This time, Lestrade raised an eyebrow.

We spent just a few short minutes with Hardwicke. He was distraught and hardly acted as if he were lying. Of course, his current accommodations were not the finest.

"Oh, Mr Holmes, I am so glad to see you. I haven't been allowed to contact anyone. I am so happy that Elizabeth had the good sense to seek you out!"

"She's seems quite a remarkable woman."

"Indeed, she is. And now she's caught up in this shameful affair."

"I should like to hear the account of 'this shameful affair' in your own words, Mr Hardwicke."

James Hardwicke gave a vivid portrayal of the events of the previous evening. Holmes listened quietly, interrupting only twice to clarify a point. While Mr Hardwicke's recount was in far greater detail than Miss Whittingham's, I shall not recount it here since it varied not once in its particulars from his fiancée's.

We left young Hardwicke promising to do all that we could for him. I must say that my heart poured out for him, for he seemed so sincere, yet I had little hope of bringing him the kind of news he was so anxious to hear.

Lestrade asked for permission to join us and Holmes readily agreed. When we arrived at the Hardwicke manor in Kensington, we were greeted by the manservant whom Holmes corralled for a moment.

"Were you in the house at the time?" he asked.

"Yes, sir."

"In the room itself?"

"No, sir. In the pantry some way down."

"Did you hear anything?"

"I did, sir. Two gunshots in quick succession. When I arrived, Mr Smythe was on the floor. I was the first to arrive, though I cannot say what precisely happened."

"Who was in the room when you arrived?"

"Master Hardwicke, Miss Whitingham, and the suddenly late Mr Smythe."

I suppressed a grin at the butler's extremely dry sense of humor.

"No one else? Just the three of them?" Holmes continued.

"Quite so, sir."

"Thank you."

The butler then left and immediately announced us to James Hardwicke's father. The elder Mr Hardwicke joined us a moment later, offering apologies that his wife was not accompanying him. "I'm afraid she is indisposed," he said sorrowfully. "She has been to her bed since this whole affair took place. She is not taking things very well, I'm afraid."

"Watson is a doctor, Mr Hardwicke," Holmes explained. "I am certain he would not mind looking in on her if you so desire."

"Not at all," I emphasized.

Hardwicke turned to me. "Your offer is most generous, sir. I believe, however, that the best medicine you can provide her with, Doctor, would be to help your renowned colleague solve this deuced mystery."

I smiled grimly. "I shall do all in my power."

Hardwicke nodded his assent.

"Could you please direct us to the room in question?" Holmes asked.

"Oh, most assuredly, Mr Holmes. This way." Hardwicke took us through a long passageway to the study. Holmes took a quick look around.

Hardwicke then spoke up.

"I'd have shot Smythe myself. He's as crooked as his father was honorable. Look at this. Why, you can even see the carpenter's marks on the bottoms of the gun racks. If this were true mahogany and varnished the way it was ordered, you wouldn't be able to see these pencil marks. Utterly disgraceful. Now it seems we'll never get our money back and have to hire new carpenters to do this job all over again." The elder Hardwicke grumbled. "If he cheated us here, then he would have cheated us elsewhere."

"Would you mind leaving us to ourselves, Mr Hardwicke?"

"Not at all, Mr Holmes. Call Porter if you need anything."

"Thank you."

"It seems the elder Hardwicke has no love for the the deceased," I noted after our host had left.

"True enough, Watson. And if Miss Whitingham had not been so adamant about her fiancé firing the fatal shot, I should think the elder Hardwicke a suspect."

"You don't believe they might be lying to cover for him?"

"Given the circumstances, likely not. Unless the butler is also lying about the elder Hardwicke's whereabouts at the time."

Holmes made a thorough examination of the room with his lens, then noted matter-of-factly, "Not so much as a splinter out of place, Watson. I shall have to take a different tack. Call Porter and have him summon Miss Whitingham and Mr Hardwicke."

I did as Holmes suggested and we were soon together again in the den. Holmes went straight to work. Lestrade had a bemused look on his face.

"Miss Whitingham, please place us in the exact positions that you, Master Hardwicke, and Mr Smythe were in at the moment of the shooting."

"Certainly, Mr Holmes. I was standing right here, facing this way. James was here, facing this way, and Mr Smythe was here, facing this way."

She positioned Holmes in the place held by the younger Mr Hardwicke and myself as Mr Smythe, standing just a few feet away. The two men were facing each other with Miss Whitingham facing both men.

"When the shots were fired, what happened then?"

"Mr Smythe's shot missed James and James shot back immediately."

"In what direction?"

"Why, directly at Mr Smythe."

"No, I mean Mr Smythe's shot. Where exactly was he aiming?" He lifted his arm high. "Like this?"

"No, lower. The bullet should have hit that wall right where the gun rack is."

Holmes stared across the room. "And yet, there is no sign of damage. How remarkable."

"Quite," the elder Hardwicke harrumphed. "The man used a stage blank, no doubt, though I cannot see his purpose except perhaps to intimidate my son."

"Perhaps," said Holmes, though I could tell by the tone of his voice that he was quite unconvinced.

"Well, if Smythe's bullet hit a wall," Lestrade noted, "someone would have heard it. No one has made any such assertion, Holmes."

"The sound of Mr Smythe's bullet hitting something would have been drowned out by the report of Mr Hardwicke's weapon, so that proves nothing," Holmes pointed out. "Well, there is no need to hold everyone here any longer. You are all free to go once again and thank you for your help."

Lestrade, I could see, had a slight smile on his face. Whether it was the smug air of self-satisfaction or a grimace of pain that his old friend was stumped, I cannot say. "I am not convinced that I should leave you alone in a crime scene, Holmes. However, I have come to trust your judgment," the police inspector said.

"And I have come to trust your wisdom," Holmes said with a twinkle in his eye.

I suspect that no one in the room save myself understood Holmes' backhanded compliment. Lestrade certainly did not. Taking Holmes' words at face value, he simply beamed with self-importance as he left.

For his part, Holmes sat and stared at the wall with his fingers tightly curled over each other in a ball at his lips. He reminded me of a chess master contemplating his next move.

I stared quietly, wondering what would happen next. Would Holmes announce a dramatic solution or simply admit defeat? As it happened, there was a third possibility I had not foreseen.

"Watson, your service revolver, please."

Baffled, I asked as I pulled it from my pocket, "Are you going to shoot at the wall, Holmes, to see if it absorbs bullets in some magical way?"

"In a manner of speaking," Holmes replied cryptically. He then really puzzled me by completely unloading the cylinder and dumping the bullets into his pocket. After double checking to make certain the weapon was completely unloaded, he took it by the barrel with the pistol grip facing outward. Then, using it as a hammer, he proceeded to pound lightly on the wall in various places. Occasional solid thuds were interspersed with a hollow sound at different spots.

At first, Holmes' hammering seemed random, but eventually he became more deliberate. He would look under the gun rack and examining a spot that only he could determine, would then pound on that spot with a hard bang, invariably producing a heavy, solid thud. Finally, he examined the gun rack which Miss Whitingham had pointed out and something must have caught his eye. His head jerked back slightly as if he had unexpectedly discovered something. He looked down the length of the wall, his gaze stopping every now and then at some spot on the wall as if he were mentally measuring some short distance from spot to spot.

"What is it, Holmes?" I asked.

"I shall know in a moment," he replied.

Using the butt of my revolver as cudgel once more, he struck just one time beneath the gun rack. The sound was distinctly hollow. While I certainly heard the difference, its significance I could not determine.

Without turning to me, he said, "Watson, would you be so kind as to ask everyone to gather here once again?"

"What shall I tell them?"

"Tell them I have said 'Eureka.'"

When we had all gathered together, Holmes stood in front of the wall far to the right side, away from the gun rack that Miss Whitingham had pointed out. He waited a brief moment as we settled down.

"Miss Whitingham," he said, "I believe you can go on planning your nuptials."

"Oh, Mr Holmes," she cried. "You have found the vanishing bullet!"

"I have."

"Where is it then?" Lestrade asked, a bit more dubiously than Miss Whitingham, to say the least.

"Right here." Holmes held out a fisted hand, turned it over, then opened it. Sure enough, it held an obviously spent bullet.

"Holmes," I said incredulously, "if that truly is Mr Smythe's errant shot, you are certainly a magician."

"Oh, it is no doubt the bullet in question, but magic had nothing to do with it."

"What, then?" demanded the elder Mr Hardwicke.

"The key was so obvious, we almost all missed it. These carpenter's marks beneath the gun racks."

"The pencil marks of that crook Smythe's hirelings? Please, Mr Holmes, you'll have to clarify that remark," said Mr Hardwicke.

"And I shall." Holmes took out my revolver once again. "In one sense, we are fortunate that Smythe used inferior wood for, as you yourself have said, Mr Hardwicke, we would not have seen these marks in a properly varnished dark wood like mahogany. There is one here."

Holmes pointed to a carpenter's mark beneath the gun rack at the far right. He banged on the wall with my revolver at a spot just below where his finger was pointing. We all heard a solid thud. "And right there is the stud behind the wall holding up this gun rack."

He repeated his demonstration twice more with the same results. He pointed out a carpenter's mark and with my revolver, pounded at that spot. In each instance, the clunk of a wooden stud was unmistakable. He then came to the final gun rack, the one the that Miss Whitingham had pointed out.

"And here is the carpenter's mark for this rack." He banged my revolver on the wall and we all heard a much different sound—one with a hollow ring.

"That incompetent!" Hardwicke thundered. "Why, his people couldn't even hang a gun rack properly!"

"Actually, Mr Hardwicke, there are two marks on this gun rack, a second one just inches from the first. Right here." Her banged the wall in this second spot and we heard a good, solid thud once more.

"What does all of this mean, Holmes?" Lestrade asked.

"It means the bullet was here," Holmes said, pointing to the mark with the hollow-sounding thud. He lifted the rack only about half an inch and there, to our amazement, he revealed a circular hole in the wall behind the rack. He then deftly inserted the bullet in his hand into the hole.

"A perfect fit," I noted.

"Indeed, Watson. The line along the bottom of this rack that we assumed was yet another carpenter's mark was, in fact, made by the errant bullet as it nudged the rack up off its mooring hooks just enough to pass into the wall, then the rack dropped back down. A perfect hiding place. It is a shot that I'm willing to bet that even the younger Mr Hardwicke could not duplicate in a million tries despite his obvious expertise.

"And furthermore, Inspector, I'm sure you'll find that this bullet fits the caliber of Mr Smythe's pistol as well." Holmes pulled the bullet back out from the hole and dropped it into Lestrade's outstretched hand.

"I'm sure it will, Holmes," Lestrade said as he examined the bullet Holmes had just handed him. "I'll see that Mr Hardwicke is released as soon as I get the paperwork completed seeing as how this is clearly a case of self-defense."

"Tell me, Holmes," I said later on our journey home, "how was it that you happened to miss the wrongly placed 'carpenter's mark' the first time you inspected the wall and the gun racks?"

"Even I succumb to human failings at times, Watson. I was concentrating so heavily on finding the tiniest speck of damage that I simply did not see the significance of the misplaced 'mark' until later." He sighed. "My carelessness almost cost a man his life. It shall not happen again."

He checked his watch. "And unless I am sadly mistaken, we shall arrive in London just in time for the last seating at Marcini's. How does that sound for dinner?"

I could not help but agree.

THE ADVENTURE OF THE BERYL CORONET

Sir Arthur Conan Doyle

"**H**olmes," said I as I stood one morning in our bow-window looking down the street, "here is a madman coming along. It seems rather sad that his relatives should allow him to come out alone."

My friend rose lazily from his armchair and stood with his hands in the pockets of his dressing-gown, looking over my shoulder. It was a bright, crisp February morning, and the snow of the day before still lay deep upon the ground, shimmering brightly in the wintry sun. Down the centre of Baker Street it had been ploughed into a brown crumbly band by the traffic, but at either side and on the heaped-up edges of the foot-paths it still lay as white as when it fell. The grey pavement had been cleaned and scraped, but was still dangerously slippery, so that there were fewer passengers than usual. Indeed, from the direction of the Metropolitan Station no one was coming save the single gentleman whose eccentric conduct had drawn my attention.

He was a man of about fifty, tall, portly, and imposing, with a massive, strongly marked face and a commanding figure. He was dressed in a sombre yet rich style, in black frock-coat, shining hat, neat brown gaiters, and well-cut pearl-gray trousers. Yet his actions were in absurd contrast to the dignity of his dress and features, for he was running hard, with occasional little springs, such as a weary man gives who is little accustomed to set any tax upon his legs. As he ran he jerked his hands up and down, waggled his head, and writhed his face into the most extraordinary contortions.

"What on earth can be the matter with him?" I asked. "He is looking up at the numbers of the houses."

"I believe that he is coming here," said Holmes, rubbing his hands.

"Here?"

"Yes; I rather think he is coming to consult me professionally. I think that I recognise the symptoms. Ha! Did I not tell you?" As he spoke, the man, puffing and blowing, rushed at our door and pulled at our bell until the whole house resounded with the clanging.

A few moments later he was in our room, still puffing, still gesticulating, but with so fixed a look of grief and despair in his eyes that our smiles were turned in an instant to horror and pity. For a while he could not get his words out, but swayed his body and plucked at his hair like one who has been driven to the extreme limits of his reason. Then, suddenly springing to his feet, he beat his head against the wall with such force that we both rushed upon him and tore him away to the centre of the room. Sherlock Holmes pushed him down into the easy-chair and, sitting beside him, patted his hand and chatted with him in the easy, soothing tones which he knew so well how to employ.

"You have come to me to tell your story, have you not?" said he. "You are fatigued with your haste. Pray wait until you have recovered yourself, and then I shall be most happy to look into any little problem which you may submit to me."

The man sat for a minute or more with a heaving chest, fighting against his emotion. Then he passed his handkerchief over his brow, set his lips tight, and turned his face towards us.

"No doubt you think me mad?" said he.

"I see that you have had some great trouble," responded Holmes.

"God knows I have!—a trouble which is enough to unseat my reason, so sudden and so terrible is it. Public disgrace I might have faced, although I am a man whose character has never yet borne a stain. Private affliction also is the lot of every man; but the two coming together, and in so frightful a form, have been enough to shake my very soul. Besides, it is not I alone. The very noblest in the land may suffer unless some way be found out of this horrible affair."

"Pray compose yourself, sir," said Holmes, "and let me have a clear account of who you are and what it is that has befallen you."

"My name," answered our visitor, "is probably familiar to your ears. I am Alexander Holder, of the banking firm of Holder & Stevenson, of Threadneedle Street."

The name was indeed well known to us as belonging to the senior partner in the second largest private banking concern in the City of London. What could have happened, then, to bring one of the foremost citizens of London to this most pitiable pass? We waited, all curiosity, until with another effort he braced himself to tell his story.

"I feel that time is of value," said he; "that is why I hastened here when the police inspector suggested that I should secure your co-operation. I came to Baker Street by the Underground and hurried from there on foot, for the cabs go slowly through this snow. That is why I was so out of breath, for I am a man who takes very little exercise. I feel better now, and I will put the facts before you as shortly and yet as clearly as I can.

"It is, of course, well known to you that in a successful banking business as much depends upon our being able to find remunerative investments for our funds as upon our increasing our connection and the number of our depositors. One of our most lucrative means of laying out money is in the shape of loans, where the security is unimpeachable. We have done a good deal in this direction during the last few years, and there are many noble families to whom we have advanced large sums upon the security of their pictures, libraries, or plate.

"Yesterday morning I was seated in my office at the bank when a card was brought in to me by one of the clerks. I started when I saw the name, for it was that of none other than—well, perhaps even to you I had better say no more than that it was a name which is a household word all over the earth—one of the highest, noblest, most exalted names in England. I was overwhelmed by the honour and attempted, when he entered, to say so, but he plunged at once into business with the air of a man who wishes to hurry quickly through a disagreeable task.

"'Mr Holder,' said he, 'I have been informed that you are in the habit of advancing money.'

"'The firm does so when the security is good.' I answered.

"'It is absolutely essential to me,' said he, 'that I should have 50,000 pounds at once. I could, of course, borrow so trifling a sum ten times over from my friends, but I much prefer to make it a matter of business and to carry out that business myself. In my position you can readily understand that it is unwise to place one's self under obligations.'

"'For how long, may I ask, do you want this sum?' I asked.

"'Next Monday I have a large sum due to me, and I shall then most certainly repay what you advance, with whatever interest you think it right to charge. But it is very essential to me that the money should be paid at once.'

"'I should be happy to advance it without further parley from my own private purse,' said I, 'were it not that the strain would be rather more than it could bear. If, on the other hand, I am to do it in the name of the firm, then in justice to my partner I must insist that, even in your case, every businesslike precaution should be taken.'

"'I should much prefer to have it so,' said he, raising up a square, black Morocco case which he had laid beside his chair. 'You have doubtless heard of the Beryl Coronet?'

"'One of the most precious public possessions of the empire,' said I.

"'Precisely.' He opened the case, and there, imbedded in soft, flesh-coloured velvet, lay the magnificent piece of jewellery which he had named. 'There are thirty-nine enormous beryls,' said he, 'and the price of the gold chasing is incalculable. The lowest estimate would put the worth of the coronet at double the sum which I have asked. I am prepared to leave it with you as my security.'

"I took the precious case into my hands and looked in some perplexity from it to my illustrious client.

"'You doubt its value?' he asked.

"'Not at all. I only doubt—'

"'The propriety of my leaving it. You may set your mind at rest about that. I should not dream of doing so were it not absolutely certain that I should be able in four days to reclaim it. It is a pure matter of form. Is the security sufficient?'

"'Ample.'

"'You understand, Mr Holder, that I am giving you a strong proof of the confidence which I have in you, founded upon all that I have heard of you. I rely upon you not only to be discreet and to refrain from all gossip upon the matter but, above all, to preserve this coronet with every possible precaution because I need not say that a great public scandal would be caused if any harm were to befall it. Any injury to it would be almost as serious as its complete loss, for there are no beryls in the world to match these, and it would be impossible to replace them. I leave it with you, however, with every confidence, and I shall call for it in person on Monday morning.'

"Seeing that my client was anxious to leave, I said no more but, calling for my cashier, I ordered him to pay over fifty 1000 pound notes. When I was alone once more, however, with the precious case lying upon the table in front of me, I could not but think with some misgivings of the immense responsibility which it entailed upon me. There could be no doubt that, as it was a national possession, a horrible scandal would ensue if any misfortune should occur to it. I already regretted having ever consented to take charge of it. However, it was too late to alter the matter now, so I locked it up in my private safe and turned once more to my work.

"When evening came I felt that it would be an imprudence to leave so precious a thing in the office behind me. Bankers' safes had been forced before now, and why should not mine be? If so, how terrible would be the position in which I should find myself! I determined, therefore, that for the next few days I would always carry the case backward and forward with me, so that it might never be really out of my reach. With this intention, I called a cab and drove out to my house at Streatham, carrying the jewel with me. I did not breathe freely until I had taken it upstairs and locked it in the bureau of my dressing-room.

"And now a word as to my household, Mr Holmes, for I wish you to thoroughly understand the situation. My groom and my page sleep out of the house, and may be set aside altogether. I have three maid-servants who have been with me a number of years and whose absolute reliability is quite above suspicion. Another, Lucy Parr, the second waiting-maid, has only been in my service a few months. She came with an excellent character, however, and has always given me satisfaction. She is a very pretty girl and has attracted admirers who have occasionally hung about the place. That is the only drawback which we have found to her, but we believe her to be a thoroughly good girl in every way.

"So much for the servants. My family itself is so small that it will not take me long to describe it. I am a widower and have an only son, Arthur. He has been a disappointment to me, Mr Holmes—a grievous disappointment. I have no doubt that I am myself to blame. People tell me that I have spoiled him. Very likely I have. When my dear wife died I felt that he was all I had to love. I could not bear to see the smile fade even for a moment from his face. I have never denied him a wish. Perhaps it would have been better for both of us had I been sterner, but I meant it for the best.

"It was naturally my intention that he should succeed me in my business, but he was not of a business turn. He was wild, wayward, and, to speak the truth, I could not trust him in the handling of large sums of money. When he was young he became a member of an aristocratic club, and there, having charming manners, he was soon the intimate of a number of men with long purses and expensive habits. He learned to play heavily at cards and to squander money on the turf, until he had again and again to come to me and implore me to give him an advance upon his allowance, that he might settle his debts of honour. He tried more than once to break away from the dangerous company which he was keeping, but each time the influence of his friend, Sir George Burnwell, was enough to draw him back again.

"And, indeed, I could not wonder that such a man as Sir George Burnwell should gain an influence over him, for he has frequently brought him to my house, and I have found myself that I could hardly resist the fascination of his manner. He is older than Arthur, a man of the world to his finger-tips, one who had been everywhere, seen everything, a brilliant talker, and a man of great personal beauty. Yet when I think of him in cold blood, far away from the glamour of his presence, I am convinced from his cynical speech and the look which I have caught in his eyes that he is one who should be deeply distrusted. So I think, and so, too, thinks my little Mary, who has a woman's quick insight into character.

"And now there is only she to be described. She is my niece; but when my brother died five years ago and left her alone in the world I adopted her, and have looked upon her ever since as my daughter. She is a sunbeam in my house—sweet, loving, beautiful, a wonderful manager and housekeeper, yet as tender and quiet and gentle as a woman could be. She is my right hand. I do not know what I could do without her. In only one matter has she ever gone against my wishes. Twice my boy has asked her to marry him, for he loves her devotedly, but each time she has refused him. I think that if anyone could have drawn him into the right path it would have been she, and that his marriage might have changed his whole life; but now, alas! it is too late—forever too late!

"Now, Mr Holmes, you know the people who live under my roof, and I shall continue with my miserable story.

"When we were taking coffee in the drawing-room that night after dinner, I told Arthur and Mary my experience, and of the precious treasure which we had under our roof, suppressing only the name of my client. Lucy Parr, who had brought in the coffee, had, I am sure, left the room; but I cannot swear that the door was closed. Mary and Arthur were much interested and wished to see the famous coronet, but I thought it better not to disturb it.

"'Where have you put it?' asked Arthur.

"'In my own bureau.'

"'Well, I hope to goodness the house won't be burgled during the night.' said he.

"'It is locked up,' I answered.

"'Oh, any old key will fit that bureau. When I was a youngster I have opened it myself with the key of the box-room cupboard.'

"He often had a wild way of talking, so that I thought little of what he said. He followed me to my room, however, that night with a very grave face.

"'Look here, dad,' said he with his eyes cast down, 'can you let me have 200 pounds?'

"'No, I cannot!' I answered sharply. 'I have been far too generous with you in money matters.'

"'You have been very kind,' said he, 'but I must have this money, or else I can never show my face inside the club again.'

"'And a very good thing, too!' I cried.

"'Yes, but you would not have me leave it a dishonoured man,' said he. 'I could not bear the disgrace. I must raise the money in some way, and if you will not let me have it, then I must try other means.'

"I was very angry, for this was the third demand during the month. 'You shall not have a farthing from me,' I cried, on which he bowed and left the room without another word.

"When he was gone I unlocked my bureau, made sure that my treasure was safe, and locked it again. Then I started to go round the house to see that all was secure—a duty which I usually leave to Mary but which I thought it well to perform myself that night. As I came down the stairs I saw Mary herself at the side window of the hall, which she closed and fastened as I approached.

"'Tell me, dad,' said she, looking, I thought, a little disturbed, 'did you give Lucy, the maid, leave to go out to-night?'

"'Certainly not.'

"'She came in just now by the back door. I have no doubt that she has only been to the side gate to see someone, but I think that it is hardly safe and should be stopped.'

"'You must speak to her in the morning, or I will if you prefer it. Are you sure that everything is fastened?'

"'Quite sure, dad.'

"'Then. good-night.' I kissed her and went up to my bedroom again, where I was soon asleep.

"I am endeavouring to tell you everything, Mr Holmes, which may have any bearing upon the case, but I beg that you will question me upon any point which I do not make clear."

"On the contrary, your statement is singularly lucid."

"I come to a part of my story now in which I should wish to be particularly so. I am not a very heavy sleeper, and the anxiety in my mind tended, no doubt, to make me even less so than usual. About two in the morning, then, I was awakened by some sound in the house. It had ceased ere I was wide awake, but it had left an impression behind it as though a window had gently closed somewhere. I lay listening with all my ears. Suddenly, to my horror, there was a distinct sound of footsteps moving softly in the next room. I slipped out of bed, all palpitating with fear, and peeped round the comer of my dressing-room door.

"'Arthur!' I screamed, 'you villain! you thief! How dare you touch that coronet?'

"The gas was half up, as I had left it, and my unhappy boy, dressed only in his shirt and trousers, was standing beside the light, holding the coronet in his hands. He appeared to be wrenching at it, or bending it with all his strength. At my cry he dropped it from his grasp and turned as pale as death. I snatched it up and examined it. One of the gold corners, with three of the beryls in it, was missing.

"'You blackguard!' I shouted, beside myself with rage. 'You have destroyed it! You have dishonoured me forever! Where are the jewels which you have stolen?'

"'Stolen!' he cried.

"'Yes, thief!' I roared, shaking him by the shoulder.

"'There are none missing. There cannot be any missing,' said he.

"'There are three missing. And you know where they are. Must I call you a liar as well as a thief? Did I not see you trying to tear off another piece?'

"'You have called me names enough,' said he, 'I will not stand it any longer. I shall not say another word about this business, since you have chosen to insult me. I will leave your house in the morning and make my own way in the world.'

"'You shall leave it in the hands of the police!' I cried half-mad with grief and rage. 'I shall have this matter probed to the bottom.'

"'You shall learn nothing from me,' said he with a passion such as I should not have thought was in his nature. 'If you choose to call the police, let the police find what they can.'

"By this time the whole house was astir, for I had raised my voice in my anger. Mary was the first to rush into my room, and, at the sight of the coronet and of Arthur's face, she read the whole story and, with a scream, fell down senseless on the ground. I sent the house-maid for the police and put the investigation into their hands at once. When the inspector and a constable entered the house, Arthur, who had stood sullenly with his arms folded, asked me whether it was my intention to charge him with theft. I answered that it had ceased to be a private matter, but had become a public one, since the ruined coronet was national property. I was determined that the law should have its way in everything.

"'At least,' said he, 'you will not have me arrested at once. It would be to your advantage as well as mine if I might leave the house for five minutes.'

"'That you may get away, or perhaps that you may conceal what you have stolen,' said I. And then, realising the dreadful position in which I was placed, I implored him to remember that not only my honour but that of one who was far greater than I was at stake; and that he threatened to raise a scandal which would convulse the nation. He might avert it all if he would but tell me what he had done with the three missing stones.

"'You may as well face the matter,' said I; 'you have been caught in the act, and no confession could make your guilt more heinous. If you but make such reparation as is in your power, by telling us where the beryls are, all shall be forgiven and forgotten.'

"'Keep your forgiveness for those who ask for it,' he answered, turning away from me with a sneer. I saw that he was too hardened for any words of mine to influence him. There was but one way for it. I called in the inspector and gave him into custody. A search was made at once not only of his person but of his room and of every portion of the house where he could possibly have concealed the gems; but no trace of them could be found, nor would the wretched boy open his mouth for all our persuasions and our threats. This morning he was removed to a cell, and I, after going through all the police formalities, have hurried round to you to implore you to use your skill in unravelling the matter. The police have openly confessed that they can at present make nothing of it. You may go to any expense which you think necessary. I have already offered a reward of 1000 pounds. My God, what shall I do! I have lost my honour, my gems, and my son in one night. Oh, what shall I do!"

He put a hand on either side of his head and rocked himself to and fro, droning to himself like a child whose grief has got beyond words.

Sherlock Holmes sat silent for some few minutes, with his brows knitted and his eyes fixed upon the fire.

"Do you receive much company?" he asked.

"None save my partner with his family and an occasional friend of Arthur's. Sir George Burnwell has been several times lately. No one else, I think."

"Do you go out much in society?"

"Arthur does. Mary and I stay at home. We neither of us care for it."

"That is unusual in a young girl."

"She is of a quiet nature. Besides, she is not so very young. She is four-and-twenty."

"This matter, from what you say, seems to have been a shock to her also."

"Terrible! She is even more affected than I."

"You have neither of you any doubt as to your son's guilt?"

"How can we have when I saw him with my own eyes with the coronet in his hands."

"I hardly consider that a conclusive proof. Was the remainder of the coronet at all injured?"

"Yes, it was twisted."

"Do you not think, then, that he might have been trying to straighten it?"

"God bless you! You are doing what you can for him and for me. But it is too heavy a task. What was he doing there at all? If his purpose were innocent, why did he not say so?"

"Precisely. And if it were guilty, why did he not invent a lie? His silence appears to me to cut both ways. There are several singular points about the case. What did the police think of the noise which awoke you from your sleep?"

"They considered that it might be caused by Arthur's closing his bedroom door."

"A likely story! As if a man bent on felony would slam his door so as to wake a household. What did they say, then, of the disappearance of these gems?"

"They are still sounding the planking and probing the furniture in the hope of finding them."

"Have they thought of looking outside the house?"

"Yes, they have shown extraordinary energy. The whole garden has already been minutely examined."

"Now, my dear sir," said Holmes. "is it not obvious to you now that this matter really strikes very much deeper than either you or the police were at first inclined to think? It appeared to you to be a simple case; to me it seems exceedingly complex. Consider what is involved by your theory. You suppose that your son came down from his bed, went, at great risk, to your dressing-room, opened your bureau, took out your coronet, broke off by main force a small portion of it, went off to some other place, concealed three gems out of the thirty-nine. with such skill that nobody can find them, and then returned with the other thirty-six into the room in which he exposed himself to the greatest danger of being discovered. I ask you now, is such a theory tenable?"

"But what other is there?" cried the banker with a gesture of despair. "If his motives were innocent, why does he not explain them?"

"It is our task to find that out," replied Holmes; "so now, if you please, Mr Holder, we will set off for Streatham together, and devote an hour to glancing a little more closely into details."

My friend insisted upon my accompanying them in their expedition, which I was eager enough to do, for my curiosity and sympathy were deeply stirred by the story to which we had listened. I confess that the guilt of the banker's son appeared to me to be as obvious as it did to his unhappy father, but still I had such faith in Holmes's judgement that I felt that there must be some grounds for hope as long as he was dissatisfied with the accepted explanation. He hardly spoke a word the whole way out to the southern suburb, but sat with his chin upon his breast and his hat drawn over his eyes, sunk in the deepest thought. Our client appeared to have taken fresh heart at the little glimpse of hope which had been presented to him, and he even broke into a desultory chat with me over his business affairs. A short railway journey and a shorter walk brought us to Fairbank, the modest residence of the great financier.

Fairbank was a good-sized square house of white stone, standing back a little from the road. A double carriage-sweep, with a snow-clad lawn, stretched down in front to two large iron gates which closed the entrance. On the right side was a small wooden thicket, which led into a narrow path between two neat hedges stretching from the road to the kitchen door, and forming the tradesmen's entrance. On the left ran a lane which led to the stables, and was not itself within the grounds at all, being a public, though little used, thoroughfare. Holmes left us standing at the door and walked slowly all round the house, across the front, down the tradesmen's path, and so round by the garden behind into the stable lane. So long was he that Mr Holder and I went into the dining-room and waited by the fire until he should return. We were sitting there in silence when the door opened and a young lady came in. She was rather above the middle height, slim, with dark hair and eyes, which seemed the darker against the absolute pallor of her skin. I do not think that I have ever seen such deadly paleness in a woman's face. Her lips, too, were bloodless, but her eyes were flushed with crying. As she swept silently into the room she impressed me with a greater sense of grief than the banker had done in the morning, and it was the more striking in her as she was evidently a woman of strong character, with immense capacity for self-restraint. Disregarding my presence, she went straight to her uncle and passed her hand over his head with a sweet womanly caress.

"You have given orders that Arthur should be liberated, have you not, dad?" she asked.

"No, no, my girl, the matter must be probed to the bottom."

"But I am so sure that he is innocent. You know what woman's instincts are. I know that he has done no harm and that you will be sorry for having acted so harshly."

"Why is he silent, then, if he is innocent?"

"Who knows? Perhaps because he was so angry that you should suspect him."

"How could I help suspecting him, when I actually saw him with the coronet in his hand?"

"Oh, but he had only picked it up to look at it. Oh, do, do take my word for it that he is innocent. Let the matter drop and say no more. It is so dreadful to think of our dear Arthur in prison!"

"I shall never let it drop until the gems are found—never, Mary! Your affection for Arthur blinds you as to the awful consequences to me. Far from hushing the thing up, I have brought a gentleman down from London to inquire more deeply into it."

"This gentleman?" she asked, facing round to me.

"No, his friend. He wished us to leave him alone. He is round in the stable lane now."

"The stable lane?" She raised her dark eyebrows. "What can he hope to find there? Ah! this, I suppose, is he. I trust, sir, that you will succeed in proving, what I feel sure is the truth, that my cousin Arthur is innocent of this crime."

"I fully share your opinion, and I trust, with you, that we may prove it," returned Holmes, going back to the mat to knock the snow from his shoes. "I believe I have the honour of addressing Miss Mary Holder. Might I ask you a question or two?"

"Pray do, sir, if it may help to clear this horrible affair up."

"You heard nothing yourself last night?"

"Nothing, until my uncle here began to speak loudly. I heard that, and I came down."

"You shut up the windows and doors the night before. Did you fasten all the windows?"

"Yes."

"Were they all fastened this morning?"

"Yes."

"You have a maid who has a sweetheart? I think that you remarked to your uncle last night that she had been out to see him?"

"Yes, and she was the girl who waited in the drawing-room. and who may have heard uncle's remarks about the coronet."

"I see. You infer that she may have gone out to tell her sweetheart, and that the two may have planned the robbery."

"But what is the good of all these vague theories," cried the banker impatiently, "when I have told you that I saw Arthur with the coronet in his hands?"

"Wait a little, Mr Holder. We must come back to that. About this girl, Miss Holder. You saw her return by the kitchen door, I presume?"

"Yes; when I went to see if the door was fastened for the night I met her slipping in. I saw the man, too, in the gloom."

"Do you know him?"

"Oh, yes! he is the green-grocer who brings our vegetables round. His name is Francis Prosper."

"He stood," said Holmes, "to the left of the door—that is to say, farther up the path than is necessary to reach the door?"

"Yes, he did."

"And he is a man with a wooden leg?"

Something like fear sprang up in the young lady's expressive black eyes. "Why, you are like a magician," said she. "How do you know that?" She smiled, but there was no answering smile in Holmes's thin, eager face.

"I should be very glad now to go upstairs," said he. "I shall probably wish to go over the outside of the house again. Perhaps I had better take a look at the lower windows before I go up."

He walked swiftly round from one to the other, pausing only at the large one which looked from the hall onto the stable lane. This he opened and made a very careful examination of the sill with his powerful magnifying lens. "Now we shall go upstairs," said he at last.

The banker's dressing-room was a plainly furnished little chamber, with a grey carpet, a large bureau, and a long mirror. Holmes went to the bureau first and looked hard at the lock.

"Which key was used to open it?" he asked.

"That which my son himself indicated—that of the cupboard of the lumber-room."

"Have you it here?"

"That is it on the dressing-table."

Sherlock Holmes took it up and opened the bureau.

"It is a noiseless lock," said he. "It is no wonder that it did not wake you. This case, I presume, contains the coronet. We must have a look at it." He opened the case, and taking out the diadem he laid it upon the table. It was a magnificent specimen of the jeweller's art, and the thirty-six stones were the finest that I have ever seen. At one side of the coronet was a cracked edge, where a corner holding three gems had been torn away.

"Now, Mr Holder," said Holmes, "here is the corner which corresponds to that which has been so unfortunately lost. Might I beg that you will break it off."

The banker recoiled in horror. "I should not dream of trying," said he.

"Then I will." Holmes suddenly bent his strength upon it, but without result. "I feel it give a little," said he; "but, though I am exceptionally strong in the fingers, it would take me all my time to break it. An ordinary man could not do it. Now, what do you think would happen if I did break it, Mr Holder? There would be a noise like a pistol shot. Do you tell me that all this happened within a few yards of your bed and that you heard nothing of it?"

"I do not know what to think. It is all dark to me."

"But perhaps it may grow lighter as we go. What do you think, Miss Holder?"

"I confess that I still share my uncle's perplexity."

"Your son had no shoes or slippers on when you saw him?"

"He had nothing on save only his trousers and shirt."

"Thank you. We have certainly been favoured with extraordinary luck during this inquiry, and it will be entirely our own fault if we do not succeed in clearing the matter up. With your pemmission, Mr Holder, I shall now continue my investigations outside."

He went alone, at his own request, for he explained that any unnecessary footmarks might make his task more difficult. For an hour or more he was at work, returning at last with his feet heavy with snow and his features as inscrutable as ever.

"I think that I have seen now all that there is to see, Mr Holder," said he; "I can serve you best by returning to my rooms."

"But the gems, Mr Holmes. Where are they?"

"I cannot tell."

The banker wrung his hands. "I shall never see them again!" he cried. "And my son? You give me hopes?"

"My opinion is in no way altered."

"Then, for God's sake, what was this dark business which was acted in my house last night?"

"If you can call upon me at my Baker Street rooms to-morrow morning between nine and ten I shall be happy to do what I can to make it clearer. I understand that you give me carte blanche to act for you, provided only that I get back the gems, and that you place no limit on the sum I may draw."

"I would give my fortune to have them back."

"Very good. I shall look into the matter between this and then. Good-bye; it is just possible that I may have to come over here again before evening."

It was obvious to me that my companion's mind was now made up about the case, although what his conclusions were was more than I could even dimly imagine. Several times during our homeward journey I endeavoured to sound him upon the point, but he always glided away to some other topic, until at last I gave it over in despair. It was not yet three when we found ourselves in our rooms once more. He hurried to his chamber and was down again in a few minutes dressed as a common loafer. With his collar turned up, his shiny, seedy coat, his red cravat, and his worn boots, he was a perfect sample of the class.

"I think that this should do," said he, glancing into the glass above the fireplace. "I only wish that you could come with me, Watson, but I fear that it won't do. I may be on the trail in this matter, or I may be following a will-o'-the-wisp, but I shall soon know which it is. I hope that I may be back in a few hours." He cut a slice of beef from the joint upon the sideboard, sandwiched it between two rounds of bread, and thrusting this rude meal into his pocket he started off upon his expedition.

I had just finished my tea when he returned, evidently in excellent spirits, swinging an old elastic-sided boot in his hand. He chucked it down into a corner and helped himself to a cup of tea.

"I only looked in as I passed," said he. "I am going right on."

"Where to?"

"Oh, to the other side of the West End. It may be some time before I get back. Don't wait up for me in case I should be late."

"How are you getting on?"

"Oh, so so. Nothing to complain of. I have been out to Streatham since I saw you last, but I did not call at the house. It is a very sweet little problem, and I would not have missed it for a good deal. However, I must not sit gossiping here, but must get these disreputable clothes off and return to my highly respectable self."

I could see by his manner that he had stronger reasons for satisfaction than his words alone would imply. His eyes twinkled, and there was even a touch of colour upon his sallow cheeks. He hastened upstairs, and a few minutes later I heard the slam of the hall door, which told me that he was off once more upon his congenial hunt.

I waited until midnight, but there was no sign of his return, so I retired to my room. It was no uncommon thing for him to be away for days and nights on end when he was hot upon a scent, so that his lateness caused me no surprise. I do not know at what hour he came in, but when I came down to breakfast in the morning there he was with a cup of coffee in one hand and the paper in the other, as fresh and trim as possible.

"You will excuse my beginning without you, Watson," said he, "but you remember that our client has rather an early appointment this morning."

"Why, it is after nine now," I answered. "I should not be surprised if that were he. I thought I heard a ring."

It was, indeed, our friend the financier. I was shocked by the change which had come over him, for his face which was naturally of a broad and massive mould, was now pinched and fallen in, while his hair seemed to me at least a shade whiter. He entered with a weariness and lethargy which was even more painful than his violence of the morning before, and he dropped heavily into the armchair which I pushed forward for him.

"I do not know what I have done to be so severely tried," said he. "Only two days ago I was a happy and prosperous man, without a care in the world. Now I am left to a lonely and dishonoured age. One sorrow comes close upon the heels of another. My niece, Mary, has deserted me."

"Deserted you?"

"Yes. Her bed this morning had not been slept in, her room was empty, and a note for me lay upon the hall table. I had said to her last night, in sorrow and not in anger, that if she had married my boy all might have been well with him. Perhaps it was thoughtless of me to say so. It is to that remark that she refers in this note:

"'My Dearest Uncle:—I feel that I have brought trouble upon you, and that if I had acted differently this terrible misfortune might never have occurred. I cannot, with this thought in my mind, ever again be happy under your roof, and I feel that I must leave you forever. Do not worry about my future, for that is provided for; and, above all, do not search for me, for it will be fruitless labour and an ill-service to me. In life or in death, I am ever your loving MARY.'

"What could she mean by that note, Mr Holmes? Do you think it points to suicide?"

"No, no, nothing of the kind. It is perhaps the best possible solution. I trust, Mr Holder, that you are nearing the end of your troubles."

"Ha! You say so! You have heard something, Mr Holmes; you have learned something! Where are the gems?"

"You would not think 1000 pounds apiece an excessive sum for them?"

"I would pay ten."

"That would be unnecessary. Three thousand will cover the matter. And there is a little reward, I fancy. Have you your check-book? Here is a pen. Better make it out for 4000 pounds."

With a dazed face the banker made out the required check. Holmes walked over to his desk, took out a little triangular piece of gold with three gems in it, and threw it down upon the table.

With a shriek of joy our client clutched it up.

"You have it!" he gasped. "I am saved! I am saved!"

The reaction of joy was as passionate as his grief had been, and he hugged his recovered gems to his bosom.

"There is one other thing you owe, Mr Holder," said Sherlock Holmes rather sternly.

"Owe!" He caught up a pen. "Name the sum, and I will pay it."

"No, the debt is not to me. You owe a very humble apology to that noble lad, your son, who has carried himself in this matter as I should be proud to see my own son do, should I ever chance to have one."

"Then it was not Arthur who took them?"

"I told you yesterday, and I repeat to-day, that it was not."

"You are sure of it! Then let us hurry to him at once to let him know that the truth is known."

"He knows it already. When I had cleared it all up I had an interview with him, and finding that he would not tell me the story, I told it to him, on which he had to confess that I was right and to add the very few details which were not yet quite clear to me. Your news of this morning, however, may open his lips."

"For heaven's sake, tell me, then, what is this extraordinary mystery !"

"I will do so, and I will show you the steps by which I reached it. And let me say to you, first, that which it is hardest for me to say and for you to hear: there has been an understanding between Sir George Burnwell and your niece Mary. They have now fled together."

"My Mary? Impossible!"

"It is unfortunately more than possible; it is certain. Neither you nor your son knew the true character of this man when you admitted him into your family circle. He is one of the most dangerous men in England—a ruined gambler, an absolutely desperate villain, a man without heart or conscience. Your niece knew nothing of such men. When he breathed his vows to her, as he had done to a hundred before her, she flattered herself that she alone had touched his heart. The devil knows best what he said, but at least she became his tool and was in the habit of seeing him nearly every evening."

"I cannot, and I will not, believe it!" cried the banker with an ashen face.

"I will tell you, then, what occurred in your house last night. Your niece, when you had, as she thought, gone to your room. slipped down and talked to her lover through the window which leads into the stable lane. His footmarks had pressed right through the snow, so long had he stood there. She told him of the coronet. His wicked lust for gold kindled at the news, and he bent her to his will. I have no doubt that she loved you, but there are women in whom the love of a lover extinguishes all other loves, and I think that she must have been one. She had hardly listened to his instructions when she saw you coming downstairs, on which she closed the window rapidly and told you about one of the servants' escapade with her wooden-legged lover, which was all perfectly true.

"Your boy, Arthur, went to bed after his interview with you but he slept badly on account of his uneasiness about his club debts. In the middle of the night he heard a soft tread pass his door, so he rose and, looking out, was surprised to see his cousin walking very stealthily along the passage until she disappeared into your dressing-room. Petrified with astonishment. the lad slipped on some clothes and waited there in the dark to see what would come of this strange affair. Presently she emerged from the room again, and in the light of the passage-lamp your son saw that she carried the precious coronet in her hands. She passed down the stairs, and he, thrilling with horror, ran along and slipped behind the curtain near your door, whence he could see what passed in the hall beneath. He saw her stealthily open the window, hand out the coronet to someone in the gloom, and then closing it once more hurry back to her room, passing quite close to where he stood hid behind the curtain.

"As long as she was on the scene he could not take any action without a horrible exposure of the woman whom he loved. But the instant that she was gone he realised how crushing a misfortune this would be for you, and how all-important it was to set it right. He rushed down, just as he was, in his bare feet, opened the window, sprang out into the snow, and ran down the lane, where he could see a dark figure in the moonlight. Sir George Burnwell tried to get away, but Arthur caught him, and there was a struggle between them, your lad tugging at one side of the coronet, and his opponent at the other. In the scuffle, your son struck Sir George and cut him over the eye. Then something suddenly snapped, and your son, finding that he had the coronet in his hands, rushed back, closed the window, ascended to your room, and had just observed that the coronet had been twisted in the struggle and was endeavouring to straighten it when you appeared upon the scene."

"Is it possible?" gasped the banker.

"You then roused his anger by calling him names at a moment when he felt that he had deserved your warmest thanks. He could not explain the true state of affairs without betraying one who certainly deserved little enough consideration at his hands. He took the more chivalrous view, however, and preserved her secret."

"And that was why she shrieked and fainted when she saw the coronet," cried Mr Holder. "Oh, my God! what a blind fool I have been! And his asking to be allowed to go out for five minutes! The dear fellow wanted to see if the missing piece were at the scene of the struggle. How cruelly I have misjudged him!'

"When I arrived at the house," continued Holmes, "I at once went very carefully round it to observe if there were any traces in the snow which might help me. I knew that none had fallen since the evening before, and also that there had been a strong frost to preserve impressions. I passed along the tradesmen's path, but found it all trampled down and indistinguishable. Just beyond it, however, at the far side of the kitchen door, a woman had stood and talked with a man, whose round impressions on one side showed that he had a wooden leg. I could even tell that they had been disturbed, for the woman had run back swiftly to the door, as was shown by the deep toe and light heel marks, while Wooden-leg had waited a little, and then had gone away. I thought at the time that this might be the maid and her sweetheart, of whom you had already spoken to me, and inquiry showed it was so. I passed round the garden without seeing anything more than random tracks, which I took to be the police; but when I got into the stable lane a very long and complex story was written in the snow in front of me.

"There was a double line of tracks of a booted man, and a second double line which I saw with delight belonged to a man with naked feet. I was at once convinced from what you had told me that the latter was your son. The first had walked both ways, but the other had run swiftly, and as his tread was marked in places over the depression of the boot, it was obvious that he had passed after the other. I followed them up and found they led to the hall window, where Boots had worn all the snow away while waiting. Then I walked to the other end, which was a hundred yards or more down the lane. I saw where Boots had faced round, where the snow was cut up as though there had been a struggle, and, finally, where a few drops of blood had fallen, to show me that I was not mistaken. Boots had then run down the lane, and another little smudge of blood showed that it was he who had been hurt. When he came to the highroad at the other end, I found that the pavement had been cleared, so there was an end to that clew.

"On entering the house, however, I examined, as you remember, the sill and framework of the hall window with my lens, and I could at once see that someone had passed out. I could distinguish the outline of an instep where the wet foot had been placed in coming in. I was then beginning to be able to form an opinion as to what had occurred. A man had waited outside the window; someone had brought the gems; the deed had been overseen by your son; he had pursued the thief; had struggled with him; they had each tugged at the coronet, their united strength causing injuries which neither alone could have effected. He had returned with the prize, but had left a fragment in the grasp of his opponent. So far I was clear. The question now was, who was the man and who was it brought him the coronet?

"It is an old maxim of mine that when you have excluded the impossible, whatever remains, however improbable, must be the truth. Now, I knew that it was not you who had brought it down, so there only remained your niece and the maids. But if it were the maids, why should your son allow himself to be accused in their place? There could be no possible reason. As he loved his cousin, however, there was an excellent explanation why he should retain her secret—the more so as the secret was a disgraceful one. When I remembered that you had seen her at that window, and how she had fainted on seeing the coronet again, my conjecture became a certainty.

"And who could it be who was her confederate? A lover evidently, for who else could outweigh the love and gratitude which she must feel to you? I knew that you went out little, and that your circle of friends was a very limited one. But among them was Sir George Burnwell. I had heard of him before as being a man of evil reputation among women. It must have been he who wore those boots and retained the missing geMs Even though he knew that Arthur had discovered him, he might still flatter himself that he was safe, for the lad could not say a word without compromising his own family.

"Well, your own good sense will suggest what measures I took next. I went in the shape of a loafer to Sir George's house, managed to pick up an acquaintance with his valet, learned that his master had cut his head the night before, and, finally, at the expense of six shillings, made all sure by buying a pair of his cast-off shoes. With these I journeyed down to Streatham and saw that they exactly fitted the tracks."

"I saw an ill-dressed vagabond in the lane yesterday evening," said Mr Holder.

"Precisely. It was I. I found that I had my man, so I came home and changed my clothes. It was a delicate part which I had to play then, for I saw that a prosecution must be avoided to avert scandal, and I knew that so astute a villain would see that our hands were tied in the matter. I went and saw him. At first, of course, he denied everything. But when I gave him every particular that had occurred, he tried to bluster and took down a life-preserver from the wall. I knew my man, however, and I clapped a pistol to his head before he could strike. Then he became a little more reasonable. I told him that we would give him a price for the stones he held 1000 pounds apiece. That brought out the first signs of grief that he had shown. 'Why, dash it all!' said he, 'I've let them go at six hundred for the three!' I soon managed to get the address of the receiver who had them, on promising him that there would be no prosecution. Off I set to him, and after much chaffering I got our stones at 1000 pounds apiece. Then I looked in upon your son, told him that all was right, and eventually got to my bed about two o'clock, after what I may call a really hard day's work."

"A day which has saved England from a great public scandal," said the banker, rising. "Sir, I cannot find words to thank you, but you shall not find me ungrateful for what you have done. Your skill has indeed exceeded all that I have heard of it. And now I must fly to my dear boy to apologise to him for the wrong which I have done him. As to what you tell me of poor Mary, it goes to my very heart. Not even your skill can inform me where she is now."

"I think that we may safely say," returned Holmes, "that she is wherever Sir George Burnwell is. It is equally certain, too, that whatever her sins are, they will soon receive a more than sufficient punishment."